GARDEN diary

A GREEN-THUMB GUIDE & PERSONAL PLANNER

Maggie Malone

Illustrated by Jill Ann Sutton-Filo

 Sterling Publishing Co., Inc.   New York

Designed by Judy Morgan

Edited by Jeanette Green

10 9 8 7 6 5 4 3 2 1

Published in 1992 by Sterling Publishing Company, Inc.
387 Park Avenue South, New York, N.Y. 10016
© 1992 by Maggie Malone
Distributed in Canada by Sterling Publishing
℅ Canadian Manda Group, P.O. Box 920, Station U
Toronto, Ontario, Canada M8Z 5P9
Distributed in Great Britain and Europe by Cassell PLC
Villiers House, 41/47 Strand, London WC2N 5JE, England
Distributed in Australia by Capricorn Link Ltd.
P.O. Box 665, Lane Cove, NSW 2066
Manufactured in the United States of America

Sterling ISBN 0-8069-8577-1

CONTENTS

INTRODUCTION

Wherever you live, whatever the size of your garden, this Garden Diary will become an indispensable companion. It was designed specifically for you, so that every facet of your garden year, from January planning to late-fall harvest, is at your fingertips for easy reference and comparison from year to year.

To assist you in the planning stages, consult the information provided under Succession Planting, Interplanting & Companion Planting, Intensive Planting, Annuals, Perennials & Biennials, as well as the Spring Planting Guide and the Fall Planting Guide.

The charts, How Much to Plant, and For Home Preserving, are provided to help you determine exactly how much seed you need to buy in order to provide the amount of produce you need. The Seed & Plant Orders log makes it easy to comparison-shop as well as to have a permanent record of your final orders.

Once the planning is done, it's time for action. Turn to the monthly pages. The first page of each month shows a list of suggested Things to Do, as well as space for you to write in specific activities for your garden. You will notice that the activities listed are timed for zones 5 and 6. Due to space limitations, it is impossible to list all activities for every zone, so I compromised by providing a starting list, a memory jog-

ger, if you will, for the zones covering the largest area in the United States. Zones farther north, of course, will schedule these activities later than suggested, and zones farther south will schedule them for an earlier date.

The Zone Map of average dates of last and first frosts shows the average date of the last spring frost and the first fall frost by zone. Keep in mind that these are only averages, and will vary from year to year. Write the frost-free date on the page for easy reference. All indoor plantings are timed to coincide with this date. The Spring Planting Guide lists how many weeks from sowing it takes for the plant to reach transplant size. Use this chart to schedule activities for each month. In early summer, use the Fall Planting Guide to time plantings for harvest in late fall.

The activity page for each month is followed by pages for Notes & Observations, as well as a graph page—My Garden Plot—which allows you to note any changes in your original plan.

You will also find a Seed Planting Log, a Harvest Log, and a Fruit Log, which, in addition to harvest information, provides space to record pruning and insect control. Other logs include a Soil Amendment & Fertilization Log, a Seed-Saver's Log, Perennial Planting & Division Records, and a Preserving Log.

january

Date of Last Frost _____
Weeks to Last Frost _____
Set-Out Date _____

Things to Do This Month

- Plan this year's garden. (Use the charts and information in this section.)
- Prune fruit trees, summer-blooming trees, and shrubs as weather permits.
?
- Fertilize spring-blooming shrubs.
- Check mulches.
- Keep snow build-up off evergreen branches to prevent breaking.
- Force rhubarb.
- Force chichons.
- Force bulbs.
- Clean and sharpen tools.
- Order seeds.
- Assemble flats and soil for next month's indoor planting.

_____
_____
_____
_____
_____
_____
_____
_____
_____
_____
_____
_____
_____

HOW MUCH TO PLANT

How much to plant is probably the toughest question any gardener must answer. A good place to start is: Did you have enough last year? Or too much? How often do you eat a particular vegetable? Once a day or once a week? Does your family really love this vegetable, or is it met with "Oh, no, not again!" Do you plan to store any of the harvest?

The chart below shows two methods of estimating how much to plant. The first is a general guideline of so many plants per person for eating fresh during the growing season and includes all uses. If a family member does not like a particular vegetable or fruit, you can easily adjust your planting. The second is how much to expect from a 50-foot row.

Two more charts, For Home Preserving—Canned and For Home Preserving—Frozen, will help you estimate your family's needs.

Variety	Plants per Person	Amount Needed to Plant 50 Feet	Yield
Asparagus	20	40 roots	15 pounds
Beans, dry shell	15–45	½ pound	45 pounds
Lima, bush	15	½ pound	12 pounds
Lima, pole	12–15	½ pound	26 pounds
Snap, bush	15–45	½ pound	60 pounds
Snap, pole	12–15	½ pound	76 pounds
Beets	40	2 packets	76 pounds
Broccoli	2	¼ ounce	50 pounds
Brussels Sprouts	1–3	¼ ounce	15 quarts
Cabbage	3–4	½ ounce	75 pounds
Cantaloupe	2–4	2 packets	35 fruits
Carrots	60–90	2 packets	50 pounds
Cauliflower	2–3	2 packets	30 heads
Corn, sweet	10–15	1 packet	48 ears
Cucumbers	2–3	2 packets	50 pounds
Eggplant	1–2	2 packets	60 fruits
Kohlrabi	5–6	2 packets	40 pounds
Lettuce, leaf	10–20	2 packets	35 pounds
Okra	1–2	1 packet	30 pounds
Onion seeds	20–50	2 packets	50 pounds

Notes & Observations

How Much to Plant

Variety	Plants per Person	Amount Needed to Plant 50 Feet	Yield
Onion sets	20–50	200	50 pounds
Parsnips	15–20	1 packet	50 pounds
Peas	90	½ pound	14 pounds
Peppers	1–2	½ pound	30 pounds
Potatoes	10–20	50 sets	50–100 pounds
Pumpkin	1	2 packets	145 pounds
Radishes	30–60	2 packets	50 pounds
Rhubarb	1	25 roots	150 stalks
Rutabagas	5–10	2 packets	50 pounds
Spinach	5–10	2 packets	10 pounds
Squash	1–2	2 packets	50 pounds
Tomatoes	1–2	2 packets	50 pounds
Turnips	15–30	2 packets	50 pounds
Watermelon	1	2 packets	15 fruits

For Home Preserving—Canned

Variety	Pounds of Fresh X for 1 Pint Canned	Number of Pints Wanted	Total Pounds Needed
Beans, Lima	1½ to 2½ in shell		
Snap	¾ to 1½		
Beets	¾ to 1¼		
Cabbage	1 pound (sauerkraut)		
Carrots	1 to 1½		
Corn	8 ears		
Onions	¾		
Peas	1½ to 2		
Peppers	1 to 1½		
Potatoes	2 to 3		
Pumpkin	¾		
Spinach	1 to 3		
Squash, Winter	¾		
Sweet Potatoes	1 to 1¾		
Tomatoes	1¼ to 1¾		
Turnips	1 to 1½		

My Garden Plot

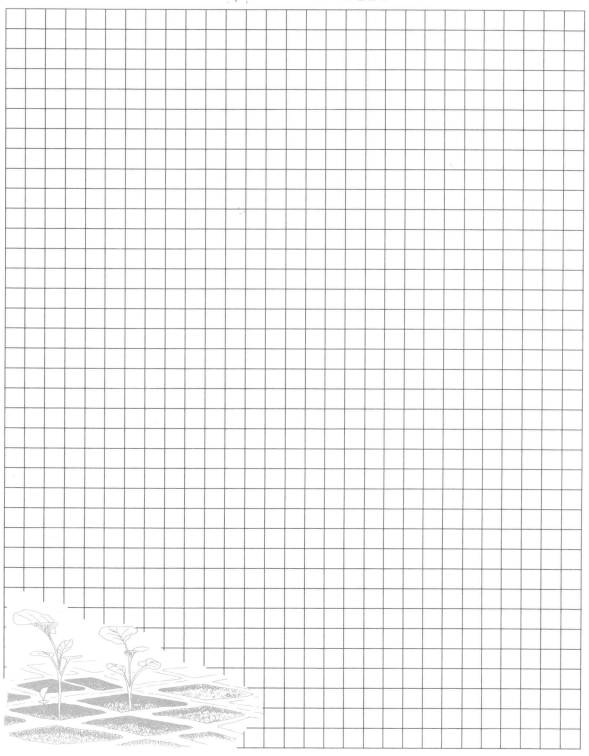

For Home Preserving—Frozen

Variety	Pounds of Fresh X for 1 Pint Frozen	Number of Pints Wanted	Total Pounds Needed
Beans, Lima	2 to 2½ in shell		
Snap	⅔ to 1		
Beets	1¼ to 1½		
Broccoli	1		
Cabbage	1 to 1½		
Carrots	1¼ to 1½		
Corn	8 ears		
Onions	2 to 3 whole		
Peas	2 to 2½ in pod		
Peppers	3 large peppers		
Pumpkin	⅔		
Spinach	1 to 1½		
Squash, Summer	1 to 1¼		
Winter	⅔		
Sweet Potato	⅔		
Tomatoes	1¼ to 1¾		
Turnips	1¼ to 1½		

Notes & Observations

Marjoram

There are three types of marjoram—sweet marjoram; wild marjoram, also known as oregano; and pot marjoram. Sweet marjoram is a tender perennial usually grown as an annual and is the one preferred for culinary use. It is a bushy plant that grows up to 1 foot high with fuzzy, pale, gray green leaves. Its tiny white or pink flowers appear in spikes in August and September.

Pot marjoram is the one preferred for medicinal use, and it is the only one that is reliably winter-hardy in colder climates. It is an erect plant that reaches heights of from 1 to 3 feet, but it does tend to sprawl. It closely resembles the oreganos.

Species name ?

CULTIVATION

For *sweet marjoram*, sow seeds in early spring indoors. Plant the marjoram seedlings outside after all danger of frost, spacing plants 6 to 8 inches apart in a medium-rich soil with plenty of humus. The site should be warm and sheltered. Pinch plants back once to encourage bushiness. Roots may be dug up and potted for indoor growth during the winter, then returned to the garden the following spring.

Pot marjoram seeds can be sown in the spring, or you can take stem or root cuttings. Plant the cuttings in a moist medium and set them outside when roots are established. Even though pot marjoram is winter-hardy, it will do better if you pot the plant and bring it indoors during the winter. It will grow and produce fresh marjoram all winter long.

HARVEST

Leaves of both varieties should be harvested in late summer, before the flower buds open. Spread the stems on screens in a dark place to dry. Marjoram retains its full flavor better than any other herb, but sunlight will rob the leaves of both color and flavor. When they are dry, store the leaves in airtight containers.

Date of Last Frost _____

Weeks to Last Frost _____

Set-Out Date _____

Things to Do This Month

- Order seeds and plants if not already done.
- Clean up winter debris.
- Continue dormant pruning.
- Apply dormant pest controls to fruit trees.
- Take cuttings of geraniums.

✳ • Sow indoors seeds requiring up to 12 weeks to transplant.

Onions
Plant chives outside. End of February.

Seed & Plant Orders

Variety	Days to Maturity	Source	Price

Notes & Observations

Seed Planting Log

Variety	Sow Directly	Cold Frame or Nursery Bed	Transplant to Garden

My Garden Plot

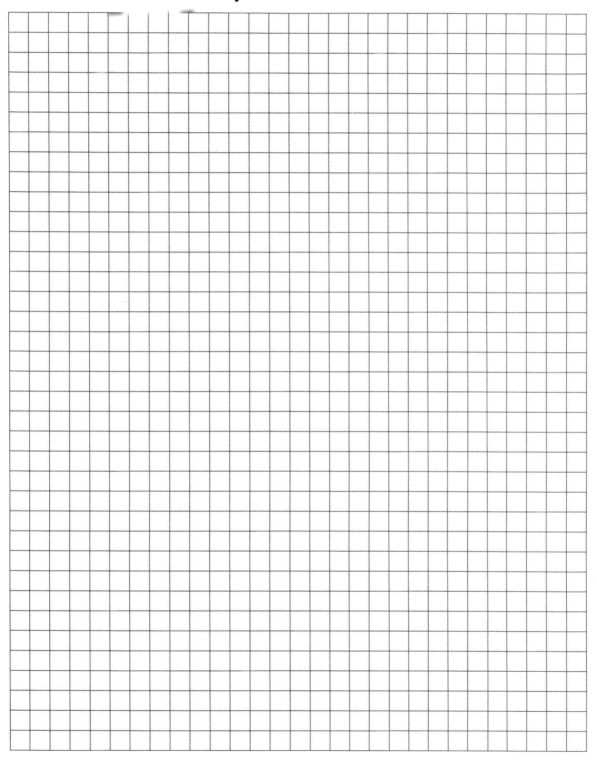

Seed Planting Log

Variety	Date Sown Indoors	Transplant to Larger Pot	Harden Off	Set Out

Notes & Observations

Caraway

Caraway, a member of the *umbelliferae* family and native to the Middle East, Asia, and Central Europe, has been in use since Mesolithic times. What would sauerkraut be without caraway? Or rye bread? As a folk remedy, caraway was used to treat flatulence, indigestion, and colic.

Like other members of the *umbelliferae* family, the leaves are finely divided, almost feathery, reaching a height of 2½ feet. The flowers appear in early summer in large, flat umbels and may be either pink or white. Seeds ripen about a month after the plant flowers.

CULTIVATION

Caraway prefers a cool climate, full sun to light shade, and a light, dry soil. It has a long taproot and should be planted where you want it to grow, either in early spring or after the seeds have ripened in late summer. Sow the seeds ½ inch deep, and thin them to stand 12 inches apart. The caraway plants will flower the following year.

HARVEST

Once the flowers appear and seeds begin to form, watch the plants carefully. The seed is ripe when it turns brown. Seeds can ripen overnight, and the seed heads can shatter, ruining your harvest. At the first sign of darkening, clip the seed heads, and hang them over a paper-lined tray to dry. Or simply drop the seed heads into a paper bag, and hang them in a warm, dry area. Store the caraway seeds in an airtight container.

march

Date of Last Frost _____

Weeks to Last Frost _____

Set-Out Date _____

Things to Do This Month

- Prepare ground when possible.
- Continue pruning and pest-control applications.
- Remove mulches from early bulbs.
- Clean up winter debris.
- Plant or divide rhubarb.
- Plant asparagus, strawberries, fruit trees, and berry bushes.
- Sow seeds of plants requiring 8 weeks to transplant size.

_____
_____
_____
_____
_____
_____
_____
_____
_____
_____
_____
_____
_____
_____
_____
_____
_____

Date of Last Frost _____   Set-Out Date _____

Spring Planting Guide
(Earliest Planting Dates)

Variety	Indoors *weeks to transplant size before last frost*	Set Out *before or after last frost*
Asparagus plants		2–4 weeks before
Beans, dry shell	4–6 weeks	1–2 weeks after
Fava		2–4 weeks before
Lima	4–6 weeks	1–2 weeks after
Snap	4–6 weeks	1–2 weeks after
Beets		4–6 weeks before
Broccoli★	6–8 weeks	4 weeks before
Brussels Sprouts★	6–8 weeks	4 weeks before
Cabbage★	6–8 weeks	5 weeks before
Carrots		4 weeks before
Cauliflower★	6–8 weeks	4 weeks before
Celeriac	10–12 weeks	2 weeks before
Celery★	10–12 weeks	2 weeks before
Chervil		6 weeks before
Chicory, witloof		2 weeks after
Chives		6 weeks before
Chinese Cabbage★	6–8 weeks	4 weeks before
Collard		4 weeks before
Corn, sweet	4 weeks	2–3 weeks after
Corn Salad		6 weeks before
Cress, upland		6 weeks before
Cucumbers	4–5 weeks	2 weeks after
Dandelion	4–6 weeks	6 weeks before
Dill		anytime after
Eggplant★	8–12 weeks	2 weeks after
Endive	4–6 weeks	4 weeks before
Fennel, Florence		4 weeks before
Garlic	Fall is best	2–4 weeks before
Horseradish plants		4–6 weeks before

★Indicates transplants: Sow seed indoors as indicated in the first column, transplant to garden as indicated in the second column.

Notes & Observations

1st wk march ⟶ plant carrots, broccoli, fennel
kale/parsley, potatoes, spinach

Spring Planting Guide
(Earliest Planting Dates)

Variety	Indoors *weeks to transplant size before last frost*	Set Out *before or after last frost*
Kale	4–6 weeks	5 weeks before
Kohlrabi	4–6 weeks	5 weeks before
Leeks★	8–12 weeks	5 weeks before
Lettuce, head★	8 weeks	2 weeks before
Lettuce, leaf★	4 weeks	2 weeks before
Melons	3–5 weeks	1 week after
Mustard	3–4 weeks	5 weeks before
New Zealand Spinach		frost-free date
Okra		2 weeks after
Onions★, plants		6 weeks before
seeds	8–12 weeks	6 weeks before
sets		6 weeks before
Parsley★	6–8 weeks	4 weeks before
Parsnips		4 weeks before
Peas, Black-Eyed		2 weeks after
Garden	3–4 weeks	6 weeks before
Peppers★	6–8 weeks	2 weeks after
Potatoes		2–4 weeks before
Pumpkins	6–8 weeks	2 weeks after
Radishes		6 weeks before
Rhubarb plants		6 weeks before
Rutabaga		2 weeks before
Salsify		4 weeks before
Shallot		6 weeks before
Sorrel		4 weeks before
Spinach		4 weeks before
Squash		2 weeks after
Sweet Potato plants		2 weeks after
Swiss Chard		2 weeks before
Tomatoes★	6–12 weeks	1 week after
Turnips		6 weeks before

★*Indicates transplants. Sow seed indoors as indicated in the first column; transplant to garden as indicated in the second column.*

Notes & Observations

Soil Amendment & Fertilization Log

Location	Amendment	Fertilizer

Notes & Observations

My Garden Plot

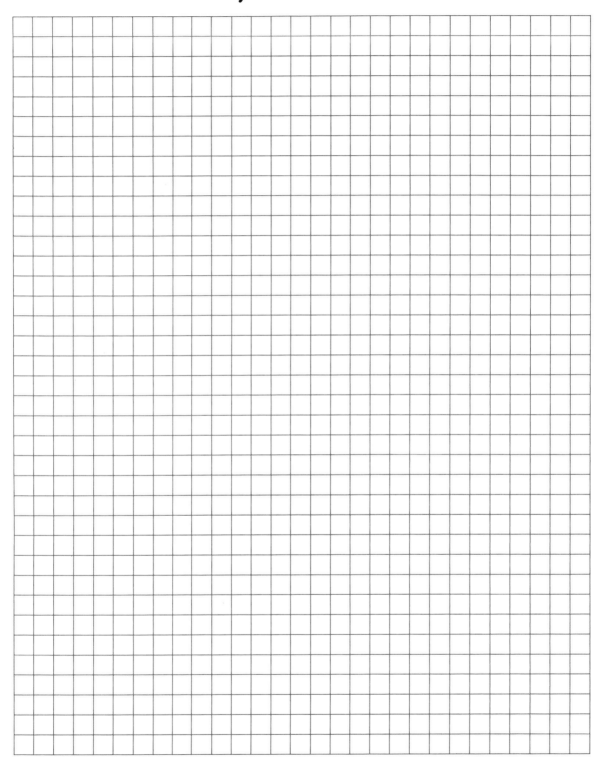

Feverfew

Biennial or perennial—zone 5
Easy

As its name implies, *feverfew* was used in ancient Greece to combat fevers. At one time or another, it has been used to treat everything from arthritis to vertigo. Modern studies have borne out its effectiveness in alleviating the pain of migraine headaches and arthritis, since it contains some of the same properties as aspirin. It also seems to be an effective insect repellant. Bees will not go near it, so be sure to place it away from any plants that you want bees to visit. Rubbing the leaves on insect bites and stings does offer some relief.

Chrysanthemum parthenium (its scientific name) is a member of the *compositae* family and its leaves resemble those broad and lobed leaves of the garden chrysanthemum. The plant grows to a height of 2½ feet with white, daisy-like flowers that bloom from June to August.

CULTIVATION

Feverfew is not at all fussy about soil. It prefers full sun but will tolerate some shade. Sow seeds indoors in flats in February or March, and transplant outside in June, spacing plants 9 to 12 inches apart. In mild areas, seed can be sown outdoors in early spring or fall.

Feverfew can also be propagated by division in early spring or by cuttings taken from October to May. For cuttings, take a heel of the old plant, along with the new growth from the base of the plant. Shorten the leaves by 3 inches and plant them in a shady spot until they root.

HARVEST

Leaves can be harvested any time throughout the growing season. Feverfew flowers are nice in herb and flower arrangements. The leaves also produce a greenish yellow dye.

Dill

Dill, a member of the *umbelliferae* family, has uses dating back at least 5,000 years to ancient Egypt, although our English word *dill* comes from the Norse language and means "to lull." This describes its ancient use as a light sedative to induce sleep. One of its more colorful uses was to ward off witches. Today, it is used primarily as a flavoring agent, imparting its pungent flavor to salads, fish, potatoes, breads, and of course, dill pickles.

The leaves, which can be used fresh, are bright green, finely divided, and feathery in appearance. The flowers are yellow and borne in large umbels up to 6 inches across.

CULTIVATION

Dill grows well in just about any soil as long as it is well drained. Seed should be sown in situ, in early spring. Dill matures quickly; so it should be sown every six weeks throughout the summer to ensure a constant supply. Thin seedlings to stand 10 to 12 inches apart. Dill supposedly self-sows, but my experience does not bear this out. I have always found it necessary to sow the seeds. Seed can also be sown in the fall; then it will germinate in early spring as soon as conditions are suitable.

HARVEST

Clip the leaves close to the stem once the plants are about 8 inches high. The seeds reach maturity two to three weeks after flowering. Watch carefully because the seeds drop quickly. As soon as they start to ripen, clip seed heads and hang them over a paper-lined tray in a dark place to dry.

Both the seeds and leaves are popularly used in cooking.

april

Date of Last Frost _____

Weeks to Last Frost _____

Set-Out Date _____

Things to Do This Month

- Finish up any tasks not completed last month.
- Divide summer- and fall-blooming perennials.
- Remove mulch from beds and shrubs. Apply mulch where needed.
- Test soil and add soil amendments and fertilizer as needed.
- For succession plants, continue sowing seeds in the cold frame.
- Harden off and transplant cool-season vegetables and flowers to the garden; protect them with covers as necessary.
- Plant and transplant trees, shrubs, ground covers, and perennials.
- Start sweet potatoes for slips.
- Pot summer bulbs for transplanting in May.
- Dig and divide spring bulbs, if necessary, as foliage dies back.
- Sow seeds of those plants needing 4 weeks to transplant size.

April 4, 1996 - transplanted 3 lavender
plants to plot in curve of driveway.
1 munstedd, 1 lavandin Provence, 1 ?
dug up ugly, squat evergreen bushes from
herb plot in curve of driveway. Put in pile in the back
to use along terrace/property line with daffodils.

INTENSIVE PLANTING

Intensive planting is the practice of spacing seeds or plants equidistant in a 3- to 4-foot-wide raised bed. This method is ideal for gaining maximum productivity in the space available. It also saves work. Since proper spacing is established at planting time, the chore of thinning is eliminated, and as the plants grow, they shade the ground, inhibiting weed growth.

Traditional spacing is given on the back of the seed packet as the distance to plant between seeds and the distance between rows. There is also a notation for thinning plants after germination, or how far apart the mature plants should stand in the row. For intensive spacing, sow the seeds or transplants the distance apart indicated for mature plants. If the packet says plants should be 6 inches apart after thinning, sow seed every 6 inches in all directions.

The list below is a general guideline for spacing requirements to help you plan your garden.

Intensive Planting

Variety	Intensive Spacing in Inches
Beans, Fava	3–5
Lima, bush	4
pole	8–10
Snap, bush	3–4
pole	6–8
Beets	2–6
Broccoli	15–18
Brussels Sprouts	15–18
Cabbage	15–18
Chinese	10–12
Cantaloupe	24–36
Carrots	2–3
Cauliflower	15–18

Notes & Observations

Intensive Planting

Variety	Intensive Spacing in Inches
Celeriac	4–8
Celery	6–9
Collards	12–15
Corn	12–18
Corn Salad	4–6
Cucumbers	18–36
Eggplant	18–24
Endive	12–15
Garlic	2–6
Horseradish	8–12
Kale	8–12
Kohlrabi	6–9
Leeks	6
Lettuce, head	10–12
leaf	6–9
Mustard	6–9
Okra	12–18
Onions, bulb	4–6
bunching	2–3
Parsley	4–6
Parsnips	4–6
Peanuts	12–18
Peas	2
Peppers	12–15
Potatoes	10–12
Pumpkins	24–36
Radishes	2–3
Rhubarb	12–36
Rutabagas	6–9
Salsify	2–3
Shallot	4

My Garden Plot

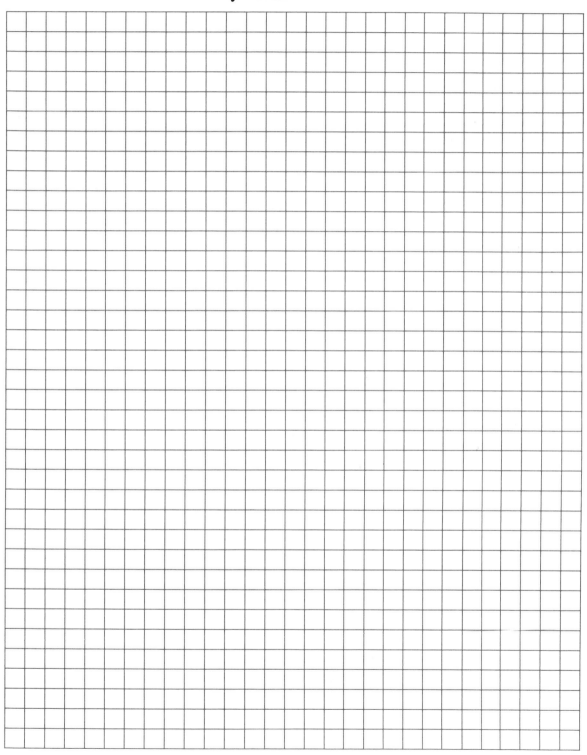

Intensive Planting

Variety	Intensive Spacing in Inches
Spinach	4–6
Malabar	8–10
New Zealand	10–12
Squash, summer & winter	24–36
Sunflowers	18–24
Sweet Potatoes	12–18
Swiss Chard	6–9
Tomatoes	18–36
Turnips	4–6
Watermelon	24–36

INTERPLANTING & COMPANION PLANTING

Interplanting is the practice of growing two crops in the space of one. Select a main crop, such as tomatoes. Plant the tomatoes the proper distance apart. Then plant a quick-growing crop, such as leaf lettuce or radishes, in the space surrounding the tomatoes. The lettuce or radishes will be harvested long before the tomatoes need the space.

Companion planting is the practice of growing two or more mutually beneficial plants in close proximity. For example, experienced farmers often grow corn and pole beans in the same area. The corn benefits from the nitrogen-fixing aspects of the beans, and the corn provides a pole for the beans to climb on.

Another reason for companion planting is to protect selected crops from insect damage. A good, all-purpose example is the marigold. The scent of marigolds is offensive to many insects, and when marigolds are spotted throughout the garden, they offer some protection from the ravages of insect damage. Marigolds also control soil nematodes.

38

Notes & Observations

Interplanting & Companion Planting

Variety	Interplant	Companion Planting
Beans, bush	Carrots, Celery, Corn, Cucumbers, Radishes, Squash	Rosemary, Catnip, Sunflowers, Celery, Potatoes
Beans, pole	Lettuce, Spinach, Corn, Squash, Tomatoes	Potatoes, Corn, Carrots, Cucumbers, Cabbage
Beets		Onions, Kohlrabi
Carrots	Lettuce, Onions, Turnips, Beans, Peas	Peas, Onions, Sage, Rosemary, Tomatoes
Celery Cole crops ?	Cabbage, Beans Squash, Cucumbers, Chives, Peppers, Dill, Carrots, Tomatoes	Leeks, Tomatoes Celery, Onions, Sage, Rosemary, Thyme, Mints, Chamomile
Corn	Beans, Peas, Lettuce, Cabbage, Potatoes	Beans, Peas, Potatoes, Cucumbers, Squash
Cucumbers	Celery, Lettuce, Okra, Eggplant, Cabbage, Squash, Corn, Chard	Radishes, Beans, Sunflowers
Eggplant	Onions	Green Beans, Potatoes
Lettuce	Beans, Cole crops, Carrots, Onions, Peas, Cucumbers, Tomatoes, Corn, Radishes, Salsify	Carrots, Radishes
Melons	Lettuce, Radishes	Corn, Nasturtiums, Radishes
Onions	Cucumbers, Carrots, Beans, Lettuce, Cabbage, Eggplant, Peppers, Spinach	Beets, Carrots

40

Notes & Observations

_____
_____
_____
_____
_____
_____
_____
_____
_____
_____
_____
_____
_____
_____
_____
_____
_____
_____
_____
_____
_____
_____
_____
_____
_____
_____
_____
_____
_____
_____
_____
_____
_____
_____
_____

Interplanting & Companion Planting

Variety	Interplant	Companion Planting
Peas	Radishes, Turnips, Cole crops, Carrots, Lettuce, Spinach	Carrots, Turnips
Parsnips	Lettuce, Radishes	
Peppers	Onions	Carrots
Potatoes	Corn	Beans, Corn, Eggplant
Pumpkin	Sweet Potatoes	Corn
Radishes	Everything	Cucumbers, Lettuce
Spinach	Onions, Kohlrabi, Radishes, Peas	Strawberries
Squash	Beans, Corn	Corn
Swiss Chard	Cucumbers	Onions
Tomatoes	Cabbage, Beans, Lettuce	Asparagus, Basil, Bee Balm, Borage
Turnips	Peas, Radishes	Peas

Thyme

If I were asked to make recommendations for the novice herb gardener, my first culinary choice would be common thyme. You can use thyme in just about everything, and all you need to do is plant it. After that, thyme requires no attention. It is a member of the mint family, so it grows quickly into a nice, large clump, although not as rampantly as the mints. Thyme reaches a height of about 12 inches. It is evergreen in warmer climates, but in my garden (zone 5), the larger stems die back, and by winter's end only a few small leaves near the ground may be seen. But thyme is one of the first plants that begins growing in the spring.

Since there are over 400 varieties of thyme, you should be able to find one that fits any situation. In form, they span the gamut from the 2-inch creeping mother-of-thyme, ideal for rock gardens, to the 12-inch upright varieties. Most thymes have a characteristic spicy scent, but you can also find lemon-, caraway-, nutmeg-, and camphor-scented thymes. The leaf colors range from the gray green of common thyme, to the shiny dark green of caraway and lemon thyme, to the variegated colors of silver thyme.

From ancient Greece until the present, thyme has been an indispensable ingredient in many medicinal potions. Its essential oil, *thymol*, is an effective antiseptic. Teas made from thyme seem beneficial for treating asthma, whooping cough, and stomach cramps. Thyme oil is used commercially in many cough medicines.

CULTIVATION

Thyme can be propagated from seed, as well as by division, cuttings, or layering. The choice is yours.

Plant the seeds indoors in early spring. Mist them daily until seeds germinate, or cover them with glass or plastic to retain moisture. When the plants are about 4 inches high, harden off, for a week, then plant them in the garden.

The plant can be divided in early spring

by digging up a mature plant and separating it into three or four pieces.

Cuttings can be taken in early spring from new growth. Cut pieces about 3 inches long, place them in wet sand, and keep them moist. They should root in about 2 weeks. Branches can also be bent over to make good contact with the soil and pegged into place. Roots will form, and the new plant can be cut from the mother plant, dug up, and transplanted to its new location.

Thyme does best in poor soil, but it must be well drained to prevent root rot and fungal diseases. Although thyme prefers full sun, it will grow in partial shade.

A winter mulch is recommended where winters are cold, but if it is in a protected area, it may not be necessary. Here in northern Ohio, I've grown common thyme for six years without ever mulching it. Some other varieties of thyme may not be reliably winter-hardy, and mulching would offer some insurance of survival.

Thyme tends to get woody as it ages; so, to keep it fresh and vigorous, clip it frequently during the summer.

HARVEST

Thyme can be clipped for use fresh any time during the spring and summer. Once established, you can cut it back to within 2 inches of the ground in midsummer. It is possible to harvest thyme twice each year, once in late spring, and again in late summer. However, the second harvest may weaken the plant just enough so that it will not survive the winter.

Hang the stems in a warm, airy place out of the sun to dry. Store thyme in airtight containers. Thyme can also be frozen.

Date of Last Frost _____
Weeks to Last Frost _____
Set-Out Date _____

Things to Do This Month

- Harvest early crops.
- Plant perennials, bare-root shrubs, and container-grown trees.
- Prune spring-flowering shrubs after flowers fade.
- Directly sow warm-season seeds.
- Transplant warm-season plants to an open garden.
- Directly sow annuals in the garden.
- Plant summer bulbs.
- Transplant bulbs planted in April.
- Pinch back mums and asters.
- Plant seeds in flats for succession plantings.

Transplant   **Sow Directly**

_____
_____
_____
_____
_____
_____
_____
_____
_____
_____
_____
_____
_____

Perennial Planting & Division Record

Variety	Date Planted	Location	Date Divided

Notes & Observations

Perennial Planting & Division Record

Variety	Date Planted	Location	Date Divided

My Garden Plot

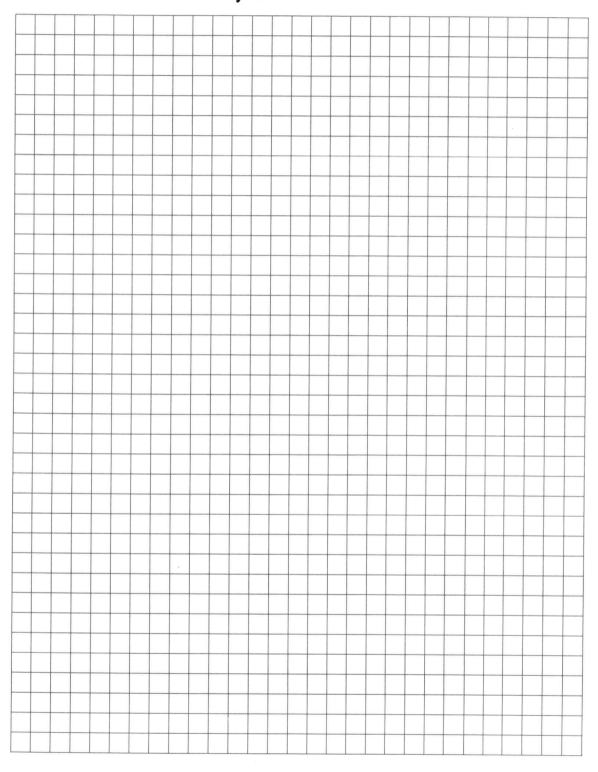

SUCCESSION PLANTING

Succession planting is the practice of re-seeding a bed as soon as a crop has been harvested. With a little advance planning, every inch of garden space remains productive from early spring through late fall, and you will harvest at least two, and sometimes even three, crops from the same space.

Draw up the plans for your garden, being sure to note the days to maturity of the vegetables you want to try. See how close this is to the first fall frost, and select varieties that will reach maturity before the ground freezes. Many of the cool-weather crops will tolerate some frost.

The list below is a general guideline to help you plan when to start plants indoors for transplanting and when you can expect a crop to be harvested so that the empty space can be filled with your ready transplants or by direct seeding.

Succession Planting

Variety	Days to Maturity
→ Beans, dry shell	60–100
Fava	80–95
Lima, bush	60–80
Lima, pole	85–90
Snap, bush	45–65
Snap, pole	60–70
Beets	50–70
Broccoli	110 (60–90 from transplant)
Brussels Sprouts	130 (85 from transplant)
Cabbage	140 (90 from transplant)
Carrots	70
Cauliflower	110 (60–75 from transplant)
Celeriac	90–120
Celery	90–120
Collards	70–80
Corn	65–90
Corn Salad	45–55

Notes & Observations

Succession Planting

Variety	Days to Maturity
Cress	30–45
Dandelion	75–90
Eggplant	120 (70 from transplant)
Endive	60–90
Florence Fennel	90
Garlic	90
Horseradish	6–8 months
Kale	60–80
Kohlrabi	50–70
Leeks	90–150
Lettuce, head	60–80
Lettuce, leaf	45–60
Melons	70–100
Onions	100–150
Parsnips	120
Parsley	80
Peas	70
Peanuts	120–140
Peppers	125 (75 from transplant)
Potatoes, white	80–140
Pumpkins	90–120
Radishes	20–60
Rutabaga	80–90
Scallions	30–40
Spinach	45–50
Squash, Summer	45–65
Winter	80–100
Sweet Potatoes	140–150
Swiss Chard	55–60
Tomatoes	120 (65–90 from transplant)
Turnips	40–75

52

Chamomile

Annual, perennial—zones 3 to 4
Easy

Chamomile, with its soft apple scent, has woven itself into the history and folklore of peoples the world over. The early Egyptians used chamomile to cure headaches and to treat fevers. Down through the ages, the gentle curative powers of chamomile were passed from culture to culture. In medieval times, it became a popular strewing herb to freshen the often disagreeable odors of unwashed bodies.

Its hardiness and the ease of caring for it, combined with its pleasant apple scent and daisy-like flowers, make it a welcome addition to the landscape. It is an outstanding ground cover. In England, it is quite common to find entire lawns sown with chamomile.

Roman chamomile is a mat-forming evergreen perennial reaching a height of 2 to 3 inches. Its light green, finely segmented leaves are borne on creeping stems that root as they spread. Yellow, button-like flowers bloom in June and July.

German chamomile, an annual, reaches a height of 15 to 18 inches. Its foliage is similar in appearance to the Roman type, but the daisy-like flowers are white. It blooms from May to October. This type has a sweeter flavor and is the one preferred for tea.

Dyer's chamomile is a highly ornamental plant, and its flowers produce a yellow dye.

CULTIVATION

Roman chamomile is not fussy about soil, but it prefers a light, dry soil in full sun or partial shade. Sow seed in early spring in a well-prepared, smooth bed, because the seed is very fine. It can also be propagated by dividing established plants and replanting the offshoots.

Sow the seed of German chamomile in September in nursery beds or where you intend it to grow. Freezing and thawing during winter increases its rate of germination. The plants will self-sow; so, it is usually necessary to sow the seeds only once.

HARVEST

The flowers of both varieties are ready to harvest when they open. They can be used fresh for teas or dried for potpourris and cosmetic preparations.

Bee Balm

Perennial—zones 4 to 9
Easy

Bee balm, native to the deciduous forests of North America, includes several varieties of mints that are attractive to bees. Indians used it as a tea and as a medication for colds and sore throats. After the Boston Tea Party, Oswego tea (_Monarda didyma_) was widely used as a substitute for black tea among the American colonists.

Besides being a soothing drink, bee balm varieties were highly prized as ornamentals. The bright, showy flowers range in color from white through pink to bright red and mahogany to lavender and purple. The flower form is striking and unusual: the petals are clustered in a whorl at the top of the stem in July and August. The strong citrus scent is most pronounced in the 6-inch-long, dark green, oval leaves. The plants grow to a height of 3 to 4 feet.

CULTIVATION

Bee balm is hardy in zones 4 to 9. The plant's natural habitat is deciduous forests, and it prefers a rich, moist humus-rich soil in partial sun or shade. Seed from a supply house can be sown in spring or summer in nursery beds and transplanted to a permanent location in the fall. Set the transplants 2 feet apart. Do not harvest the plant the first year, since it needs time to become established. Bee balm cross-pollinates quite easily, and it may not reproduce true to variety from saved seed. Bee balm grows vigorously, spreading in a circle pattern from the center outward. As the center dies out, it is necessary to dig the plants up and divide them, discarding the center portion. This is your opportunity to increase your stock.

HARVEST

The leaves and flowers can be picked and used fresh throughout the summer. In late summer, cut the stems down to within an inch of the ground. The leaves can be stripped from the stems and spread on trays to dry, or small bunches can be hung upside down in a dry, shady area. The leaves should dry within three days. If they do not, place them in a very low-heat oven to complete the drying process. If the stems are cut right after flowering, they may produce a second crop of flowers in the fall.

Date of Last Frost _____

Date of First Frost _____

Set-Out Date _____

Weeks to First Frost _____

Things to Do This Month

- Harvest.
- Fertilize.
- Plant container-grown plants and summer bulbs.
- Prune shrubs after blooming.
- Divide spring-flowering perennials after blooms have faded.
- Pinch back mums and asters a second time.
- Directly sow warm-season vegetables.
- Sow flats of cool-season vegetables for succession planting.
- Mulch beds to retain moisture.

Sow in Flats or Nursery Bed   **Sow Directly**

GUIDE FOR ANNUALS, PERENNIALS & BIENNIALS

Since annuals complete their life cycle in one year, of course they must be replanted the following year. They provide quick color in the garden to fill in while you wait for perennials to mature.

A few perennials will flower the first year from seed sown in early spring. For the majority, however, and for biennials, it is best to sow them in nursery beds in July. The seedlings can be transplanted to their permanent locations in September or spend winter in the nursery beds for transplanting the following spring.

The list of perennials (HP—hardy perennial, HHP—half-hardy perennial) and biennials (HB—hardy biennial) that follows is provided to assist you in planning your flower garden by indicating the bloom time and height of plants, as well as zone hardiness. Check your catalog for specific information on your particular variety, since some perennials, such as lupins, have varieties that are annual as well as perennial and are suitable to different zones. One hybrid lupin is hardy in zones 7 to 9 while another is hardy in zones 4 to 7. In this case, the zone is indicated as 4 to 9 to show that there are varieties suitable for this range.

HHP indicates a plant that is perennial in warmer climates but that will bloom the same year from seed in colder climates, where it should be treated as an annual.

Annuals

Variety	When to Sow *weeks to transplant size*	Light	Bloom Time	Height in Inches
Acrolinium★★	6–8 (2)	Sun	S	24
African Daisy	6–8 (1)	Sun	S–F	12
Ageratum	6–8 (2)	Sun	S	5–30
Alyssum★★	8–10 (1)	Sun	S–F	3–4
Amaranthus	8 (2)	Sun	S–F	15–48
Ammi Majus★★	6–8 (1)	Sun	Sp–S	36
Anchusa★★	6–8 (1)	Sun	S	8–10

Notes & Observations

Annuals

Variety	When to Sow *weeks to transplant size*	Light	Bloom Time	Height in Inches
Arctotis★★	6–8 (1)	Sun	S–F	12
Aster★★	6–8 (1)	Sun	LS–F	6–36
Balsam	6–8 (2)	PSun	S–F	10–14
Begonia	Anytime	Shade	Anytime	10–12
Bells of Ireland★★	8–10 (1)	PSun	Sp–S	24–36
Brachycome	6–8 (2)	Sun	S–F	9
Browallia	6–8	PSun	Anytime	10
Cabbage, flowering	6–8 (1)	Sun	S–F	12
Calendula★★	6–8 (1)	Sun	Sp S W	12–30
California Poppy★★	(1)	Sun	Sp S W	12
Candytuft★★	6–8 (1)	Sun	Sp	20
Carnation★★	8–10	Sun	S	10–24
Celosia	6–8 (1)	Sun	S–F	12–40
Centaurea★★	6–8 (2)	Sun	S	16–30
Clarkia★★	(1)	Sun	S–F	20
Cleome	6–8 (1)	Sun	S–F	36–48
Coleus	6–8 (2)	PSun		8–24
Cosmos	(2)	Sun	S–F	24–48
Crape Myrtle	6–8 (2)	Sun	S	10–48
Dahlberg Daisy	6–8 (2)	Sun	S	8
Dahlia	6–8 (2)	Sun	S	18–48
Dianthus★★	6–8 (1)	Sun	S–F	7–14
Dusty Miller	6–8 (1)	Sun		7–9
Emilia★★	(1)	Sun	S–F	12–15
Euphorbia	(2)	Sun		18
Felicia★★	6–8 (1)	Sun	S–F	36
Feverfew★★	6–8 (1)	Sun	S	8
Forget-me-not★★	(1)	PSun	S	4–12
Four-o'clock	6–8 (2)	Sun	S	30
Gazania	6–8 (2)	Sun	S–F	8–12

My Garden Plot

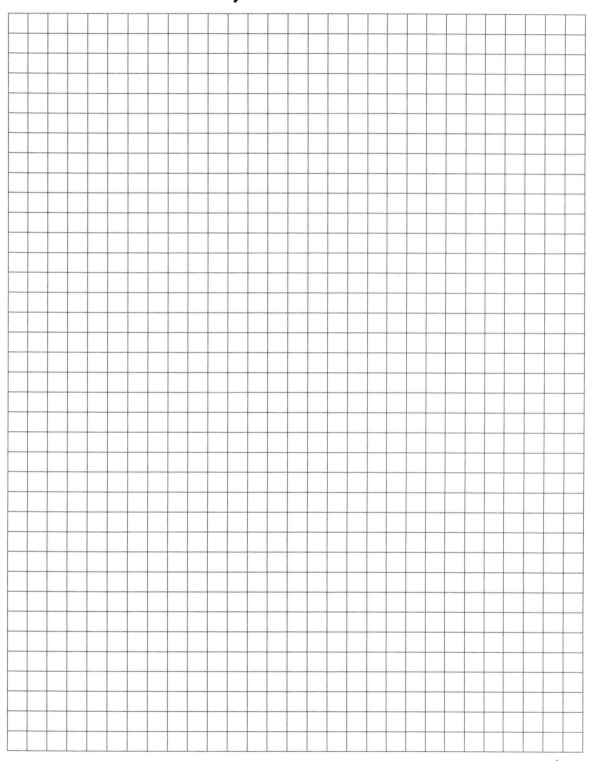

Annuals

Variety	When to Sow _weeks to transplant size_	Light	Bloom Time	Height in Inches
Geranium	10–12 (2)	Sun	S–F	12–18
Gomphrena	6–8 (2)	Sun	S–F	6–15
Gypsophila★★	6–8 (1)	Sun	S	30
Helichrysum★★	6–8 (1)	Sun	S	12–30
Heliotrope	6–8 (2)	PSun	S–F	15
Hollyhock★★	6–8 (1)	Sun	S	36–40
Impatiens	8–12 (2)	Shade/PSun	S–F	12
Kochia	6–8 (2)	Sun		24–30
Larkspur★★	6–8 (1)	Sun	S	48–60
Lavatera★★	6–8 (1)	Sun	S–F	24
Linaria★★	6–8 (1)	Sun	S–F	8
Lobelia★★	8–10 (1)	PSun	S–F	4–6
Marigold	2–3 (2)	Sun	S–F	6–36
Mignonette	2–3 (2)	Shade/PSun	S	12
Mimulus	10–12	PSun	S	10
Morning Glory	6–8 (2)	Sun	S	Vine
Nasturtium	2–3 (2)	Sun	S	6–36
Nemesia	2–3 (2)	Sun	Sp–S	24
Nemophila★★	6–8 (1)	Shade/S	Sp	10
Nicotiana	6–8 (2)	Shade/PSun	S–F	24–30
Nierembergia	6–8 (2)	Shade/PSun	S–F	6
Nigella	6–8 (2)	Sun	S	24–36
Pansy★	8–10 (1)	PSun	Sp–F	7
Periwinkle	6–8 (2)	Sun	S	6–15
Petunia	6–8 (2)	Sun	S–F	8–15
Phlox★★	6–8 (1)	Sun	S	8
Poppy★★	(1)	Sun	S	10–24
Portulaca	6–8 (2)	Sun	S–F	6–8
Salpiglossis★★	8–10 (1)	Sun	S–F	30
Salvia	6–8 (2)	Sun	S–F	8–18

Notes & Observations

_____
_____
_____
_____
_____
_____
_____
_____
_____
_____
_____
_____
_____
_____
_____
_____
_____
_____
_____
_____
_____
_____
_____
_____
_____
_____
_____
_____
_____
_____
_____
_____
_____
_____

Annuals

Variety	When to Sow *weeks to transplant size*	Light	Bloom Time	Height in Inches
Sanvitalia	6–8 (2)	Sun	S–F	8
Scabiosa★★	2–3 (2)	Sun	S–F	18–36
Snapdragon	8–10 (2)	Sun	S	18–36
Statice	6–8 (2)	Sun	S–F	24–36
Stock★★	6–8 (2)	Sun	S–F	8–18
Sunflower	2–3 (2)	Sun	S–F	36–60
Sweet Pea	6–8 (1)	Sun	Sp/F	Vine
Tithonia	2–3 (2)	Sun	S–F	24–48
Verbena	2–3 (2)	Sun	S–F	9–12

★*This half-hardy perennial can winter in a cold frame or be mulched for early-spring bloom. This plant is perennial in the Southern states and should be sown in the fall.*
★★*The plant prefers cool temperatures, and it can be planted in the fall in the South.*
(1) recommends that you transplant or directly sow the plant after the last heavy frost, while the ground is still cool.
(2) recommends that you transplant or directly sow the plant after all danger of frost has passed and when the ground has warmed.

Perennials & Biennials

Variety	Type	Light	Zone	Flower	Height in Inches
Acanthus	HP	PShade	8–9	S	36
Achillea	HP	Sun		Sp–F	8–60
Aconitum	HP	PShade	3–8	S–F	24–48
Alyssum	HP	Sun	3–8	Sp–S	4–12
Alchemilla	HP	Sun	3–8	S	6–18
Anacyclus	HP	Sun	6–10	LSp	3
Anaphalis	HP	Sun	3–8	LS	12–18
Anthemis	HP	Sun	4–9	S–F	6–24
Aquilegia	HP	PSun	3–9	Sp–S	6–30
Arabis	HP	Sun	3–7	Sp	4–6

Notes & Observations

Perennials & Biennials

Variety	Type	Light	Zone	Flower	Height in Inches
Armeria	HP	Sun	3–8	S	6–24
Arnica	HP	PShade	3–8	S	12–15
Asclepias	HP	Sun	3–9	S	12–36
Aster	HP	Sun	4–8	S–F	12–48
Astilbe	HP	Shade	5–8	S	6–12
Aubretia	HP	Sun	4–9	Sp	4
Begonia	HHP	Shade		Sp–S	10–15
Belamcanda	HP	Sun	5–10	S	36–40
Bellis	HB	PSun	3–9	LSp	4–8
Bergenia	HP	PShade	4–9	Sp	12
Berlandiera	HHP	Sun		S	18
Bupthalmum	HP	Sun	3–8	Sp–F	24–72
Caltha	HP	Sun	3–9	Sp	12–15
Campanula	HP	PShade	3–9	S	4–48
Campanula	HB	PShade	3–9	S	30–48
Candytuft	HP	Sun	4–9	Sp–S	9
Canna	HHP	Sun	3–8	S	36
Catananche	HP	Sun	4–9	S	24
Centaurea	HP	Sun	3–9	S	24
Centranthus	HP	Sun	4–9	S–F	18
Cephalaria	HP	Sun/PShade	3–9	S	60
Cerastium	HP	Sun	3–9	LSp	6
Chelone	HP	Sun	3–9	S–F	18–24
Chiastophyllum	HP	Sun/PSun	4–8	S	9
Chrysanthemum	HP	Sun	4–10	LS–F	12–36
Cimicifuga	HP	Shade	3–9	LS	36–60
Clematis	HP	Sun	3–9	Sp–S–F	Vine
Coreopsis	HP	Sun	3–10	S–F	12–18
Cynara	HP	Sun	8–10	S–F	48
Cyclamen	HP	PShade	4–7	S–F	3–6

Continued on p. 68.

Comfrey

If you're new to herbs and want to build your confidence, this is the plant for you. Success is assured since it is impossible to kill comfrey. If you try, whether through ignorance or clumsiness, all you get is more comfrey.

And therein lies a warning: Once you have comfrey growing, you will never get rid of it. Any piece of root, no matter how small, will grow a comfrey plant. So, use care when selecting its location since it will overwhelm other plants in its vicinity.

However, since comfrey is such a handsome plant, it is well worth growing for its appearance alone. Pinkish purple flowers are set off by the broad, 10-inch-long dark green leaves. The plant will reach a height of 3 to 5 feet, which makes it a perfect background plant.

Not only is it a handsome plant, but its medicinal properties are legendary. Comfrey has been a staple in healing arts since about 400 B.C., and modern scientific studies have borne out many of its claims. Both the leaves and roots of comfrey contain *allantoin*, a healing compound found to accelerate healing by stimulating new tissue growth. It also kills bacteria and has been used to treat infections. Historically, the crushed root was used to treat broken bones, hence one of its nicknames, *knitbone*. By grinding the fresh leaves and applying them to the skin, you will promote the growth of new cells while making the skin soft and smooth. The dried root can be ground, mixed with hot water (not boiling), and applied to the skin to promote the healing of insect bites, skin problems, bruises, sprains, and burns.

At one time, comfrey was taken internally for medicinal purposes and was widely used as a food source. Studies done during the 1970s, however, indicate that it could cause cancer; so, its use internally is no longer recommended.

CULTIVATION

Comfrey can be grown from seed, cuttings, or root division—the easiest way being a root cutting.

I have not seen seeds listed in mail-order catalogs, but root cuttings are readily available. A root cutting can be planted in a moist, rich soil, in sun or part shade, at any time during the growing season. Space plants three feet apart. Once planted, comfrey requires no special care.

HARVEST

During the growing season, the leaves contain the highest concentration of allantoin; therefore, use the leaves fresh for skin lotions or dry the leaves and store them until needed. Steep the dried leaves in hot water. The rhizome can also be dug up and dried. When ready to use, grind the rhizome and mix it with hot water.

65

Oregano

Perennial–zone 5
Easy

Oregano and marjoram are often confused, even by botanists, and some question whether they are two separate species or merely different forms of the same species. *Origanum vulgare*, or common oregano, grows to 2 feet in height with oval to pointed leaves up to 2 inches long. The flowers appear in terminal spikes from July to September.

Oregano is native to the mountains of Greece. We know it as the indispensable herb in pizza and Italian dishes, but its early uses were primarily medicinal. A tea was made to treat chronic coughs and asthma; the oil was used to treat toothaches.

CULTIVATION

Grow oregano from a plant or division. Select *Origanum heracleoticum* for best flavor. Plant in a rich, light, well-drained soil in full sun.

HARVEST

The leaves can be harvested when the plant is quite young. In fact, the harvest encourages new growth, which makes the plant bushy. Just before the plants bloom, cut them back to within 2 inches of the ground and again in late summer to encourage new growth. Oregano also makes an excellent pot plant for growing indoors in winter.

Date of First Frost _____
Weeks to First Frost _____
Set-Out Date _____

Things to Do This Month

- Harvest.
- Fertilize.
- Sow seeds of biennials and perennials in nursery beds.
- Take softwood cuttings of shrubs, vines, ground covers, and houseplants.
- Order spring bulbs, roses, perennials, shrubs, and trees for fall planting.
- Divide overgrown perennials after flowering.
- Pinch back mums and asters.
- Replant harvested areas in the vegetable garden.
- Prune raspberries.

Sow in Nursery Bed or Cold Frame   **Sow Directly**

Perennials & Biennials

Continued from p. 64.

Variety	Type	Light	Zone	Flower	Height in Inches
Delphinium	HP	Sun	4–6	S	24–60
Dianthus	HHP	Sun	3–9	S	8–18
Dicentra	HP	Shade	4–8	Sp–S	12–24
Dictamnus	HHP	Sun/PSun	7–9	S	9–24
Dierama	HP	PSun	7–9	S	48
Digitalis	HB	PShade	4–9	Sp	18–60
Disporum	HP	Shade	7–9	Sp	12–36
Dodecatheon	HP	Shade	4–9	Sp–S	15–24
Doronicum	HP	Sun/PSun	4–8	Sp	12–24
Echinacea	HP	Sun	3–9	S	36–48
Echinopsis	HP	Sun	3–9	S	48–72
Epilobium	HP	Sun/PShade	4–9	S	12
Eranthis	HB	Sun/PShade	4–9	W	4
Eremurus	HP	Sun	6–9	S	24–40
Erigeron	HP	Sun	6–9	S	12
Eriophyllum	HP	Sun	6–9	S	12–24
Erynigium	HP	Sun	5–6	S	18–72
Erythronium	HB	PShade	3–9		6–16
Euphorbia	HP	Sun	4–10	S	12–36
Eustoma	HHP	Sun	5–10	S	18–24
Foeniculum	HP	Sun	4–9	S	72
Gaillardia	HP	Sun	3–9	S–F	15–24
Galega	HP	Sun	3–9	S–F	30–40
Gentiana	HP	Sun	3–9	S	4–18
Geranium	HP	PShade	3–8	S	12–24
Geum	HP	Sun	5–9	S	6–18
Gypsophila	HP	Sun	3–8	S	30–48
Hedysarum	HP	Sun	4–9	S	24–48
Helenium	HP	Sun	5–9	S	24–48
Helianthemum	HP	Sun	6–9	S	9
Helichrysum	HP	Sun	7–10	S	24–36

Notes & Observations

Perennials & Biennials

Variety	Type	Light	Zone	Flower	Height in Inches
Heliopsis	HP	Sun	4–9	S	36–48
Heliotrope	HHP	Sun/PShade		S	14–24
Helleborus	HP	PShade	3–8	W–Sp	9–18
Hemerocallis	HP	Sun/PShade	3–10	S	15–24
Hepatica	HP	PShade	4–8	W–Sp	4–6
Hesperis	HB	Sun	3–10		18
Heuchera	HP	Sun	3–9	S	12–24
Hibiscus	HHP	Sun		S	18–72
Heiracium	HP	Sun	3–9	S	12
Hollyhock	HHP	Sun	2–9	S	24–96
Hosta	HP	PShade	3–10	S	18–36
Hunnemannia	HHP	Sun		S	24
Iceland Poppy	HB	Sun		S	15–20
Incarvillea	HP	Sun	3–8	S	12–18
Inula	HP	Sun	3–9	S	24
Impatiens	HHP	PShade		S	6–12
Iris	HP	Sun	4–9	Sp	18–36
Jasione	HP	Sun	5–9	S	9–12
Knautia	HP	Sun	3–9	S	24
Kniphofia	HP	Sun	6–9	S–F	30–48
Lantana	HHP	Sun		Sp–S	18
Lathyrus	HP	Sun	3–9	S	Vine
Lavatera	HP	Sun	4–9	S	60–72
Lavender	HP	Sun/PShade	5–9	S	12–36
Leontopodium	HP	Sun/PShade	4–7	Sp	6
Lewisia	HP	Sun	4–7	Sp–S	3–9
Liatris	HP	Sun	3–10	S	24–60
Libertia	HP	Sun	9–10	S	18–36
Ligularia	HP	PShade	4–8	S	30–60
Limonium	HP	Sun	3–9	S	24
Linum	HP	Sun	5–9	S	6–18

Notes & Observations

Perennials & Biennials

Variety	Type	Light	Zone	Flower	Height In Inches
Lotus	HP	Sun	4–9	S	4
Lunaria	HB	Shade		Sp	30
Lupine	HP	Sun	4–9	Sp–S	36
Lychnis	HP	Sun	3–9	S	18–36
Lysichitum	HP	Sun	3–9	Sp	24
Lysimachia	HP	Sun	5–9	S	12–36
Lythrum	HP	Sun/PShade	3–9	S	24–48
Macleaya	HP	PSun	3–9	S	60–96
Malva	HP	S/PShade	4–9	S	24–36
Matricaria	HHP	Sun	6–10	S	3–24
Monarda	HP	Sun/PShade	4–9	S	30–36
Morina	HP	Sun/PShade	6–9	S	36–48
Myosotidium	HHP	PShade		Sp	12–18
Myosotis	HB	Sun		Sp	6–12
Oenothera	HHP	Sun	3–9	S–F	18–48
Onopordum	HB	Sun	3–9	S	72
Oregonum	HP	Sun	5–9	S	24–30
Paeonia	HP	Sun	5–9	Sp–S	24
Pansy	HHP	Sun/PShade		Sp	6–9
Papaver	HP	Sun	3–9	S	4–60
Penstemon	HHP	Sun	5–9	S	6–30
Physalis	HP	Sun	3–9	S	24
Physostegia	HP	PShade	3–9	S	24–36
Pinguicula	HP	Sun	3–8	Sp–S	3–4
Platycodon	HP	Sun	3–9	S	6–18
Podophyllum	HP	Shade	5–10	S	12
Polygonatum	HP	PShade	4–8	Sp	30
Potentilla	HP	Sun	5–9	S	4–24
Primula	HP	Sun	3–9	Sp–F	4–36
Prunella	HP	Sun	6–9	Sp–F	6–12
Psilostrophe	HP	Sun	5–8	S–F	24

Notes & Observations

_____
_____
_____
_____
_____
_____
_____
_____
_____
_____
_____
_____
_____
_____
_____
_____
_____
_____
_____
_____
_____
_____
_____
_____
_____
_____
_____
_____

Perennials & Biennials

Variety	Type	Light	Zone	Flower	Height in Inches
Pulsatilla	HP	Sun	4–8	S	4–12
Ramonda	HP	PShade	5–8	Sp–S	6
Rheum	HP	Sun	3–8	S	72
Rodgersia	HP	PShade	6–8	S	36–48
Roscoea	HP	Sun/PShade	5–8	S	15
Rudbeckia	HP	Sun	3–9	S	24–48
Salvia	HP	Sun	4–9	S	12–36
Santolina	HP	Sun	3–8	S	12–24
Saxifraga	HP	Shade	3–9	S–F	3–12
Scabiosa	HP	Sun	3–9	S	12–20
Scilla	HP	Sun	3–9	Sp–S	18
Sidalcea	HP	Sun	5–9	S	30–40
Silene	HP	Sun/PShade	5–8	Sp–S	6–18
Solidago	HP	Sun/PShade	3–9	S	24
Stachys	HP	Sun/PShade	5–9	S	12
Thalictrum	HP	Sun/PShade	4–8	S	12–60
Tradescantia	HP	Sun/PShade	6–9	S	18
Trillium	HP	Shade	3–8	Sp–S	10–12
Trollius	HP	Sun/PShade	3–8	Sp–S	3–30
Veronica	HP	Sun/PShade	5–9	S	12–15
Viola	HHP	Sun	6–9	S	3–9
Violets	HP	Sun/PShade	6–9	S	4–9
Wallflower	HB	Sun		Sp–S	12–18
Yucca	HP	Sun	4–10	S	36–120

Notes & Observations

My Garden Plot

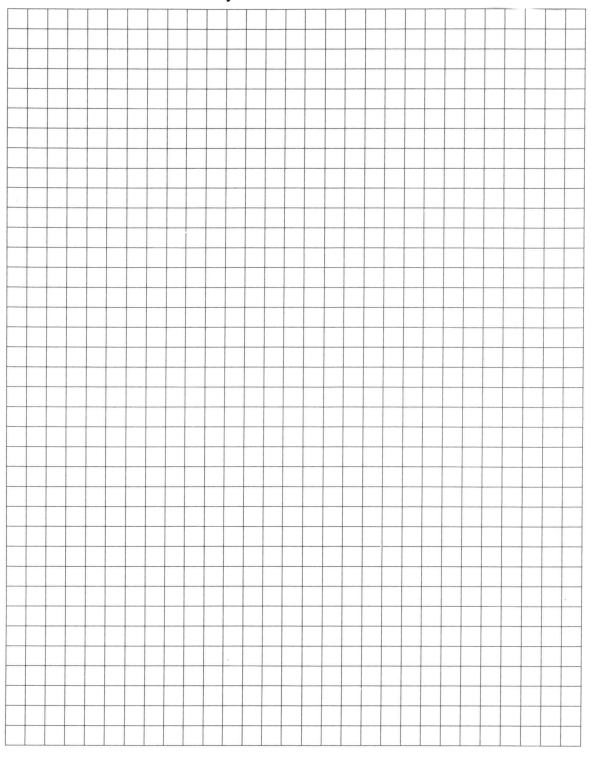

Anise

People have valued the licorice flavor of anise for centuries. The Greeks and Romans used it extensively in medicinal preparations, to freshen breath, aid digestion, relieve gas pains, and soothe coughs. The Romans prized anise so highly that it was accepted as payment for taxes. Anise was introduced to the United States by settlers in the Virginia colony, who were required by law to bring and plant six anise seeds.

Anise is still widely used to flavor cough and cold remedies and to freshen breath, and modern studies have confirmed that it helps relieve gas pains. It is popular worldwide as a culinary herb, imparting its flavor to soups and stews, fruits, cheeses, meats, baked goods, and liqueurs.

CULTIVATION

Anise is a member of the *umbelliferae* family, which includes carrots, dill, caraway, and fennel. It resembles Queen Anne's lace—the lower leaves rounded with toothed edges and the upper leaves more feathery. Large flat, whitish flower umbels appear in July and August. The plant reaches a height of 2 feet.

Because of its long taproot, members of this family are difficult to transplant and should be sown where you want them to grow. Sow the seed in full sun in average garden soil after all danger of frost has passed. Thin seedlings so that they stand 8 to 12 inches apart. The growth is spindly and easily damaged, so the seedlings should be set in an area protected from high winds and heavy rains. Once established, anise requires little care other than to be kept weed-free.

HARVEST

The seeds appear in July and August. Allow the seed heads to ripen, but be sure to harvest them before they shatter. Clip the heads into a paper bag to contain the seeds. Spread them out in the sun on trays to finish drying. Store the seeds in tightly sealed containers.

Fennel

Half-hardy perennial—zone 6
Annual or biennial in colder
zones

Fennel is another member of the *umbelliferae* family, closely related to dill, caraway, and anise. It has the same feathery leaf structure, and the small yellow flowers form large, flat umbels at the top of the stem. Fennel's licorice flavor is milder than that of anise, but it is still very pronounced. While grown primarily for its seeds, the leaves are also used fresh or dried.

Florence fennel has the same soft licorice flavor as regular fennel, but it is grown more for its large, bulbous stalks. The stalks are treated and used in much the same way as celery.

CULTIVATION

Fennel will grow in any light, well-drained soil in full sun. For an early-spring crop, sow seed in the fall, thinning to stand 6 inches apart. Sow in the spring and every six weeks thereafter for a continuous harvest.

HARVEST

The leaves can be clipped once the plants have reached a height of 6 to 8 inches. The stems of Florence fennel can be cut whenever they reach eating size. To harvest the seeds, wait until they turn brown; then clip the heads and place them in paper bags to dry. The seeds will drop into the bag. Be alert—the seeds drop quickly.

78

Date of First Frost _____

Weeks to First Frost _____

Things to Do This Month

- Harvest.
- Fertilize.
- Plant madonna lilies and move mums to permanent location.
- Transplant cool-season vegetables to the garden.
- Sow quick-growing cool-season vegetables.
- Take herb cuttings to pot for indoor use.

Sow in Nursery Bed or Cold Frame   **Sow Directly**

Harvest Log

Variety	Date	Amount

Notes & Observations

Harvest Log

Variety	Date	Amount

Notes & Observations

Fruit Log

Variety	Date Planted	Pruning Date	Insect Control	Harvest	
				Start	End

Notes & Observations

My Garden Plot

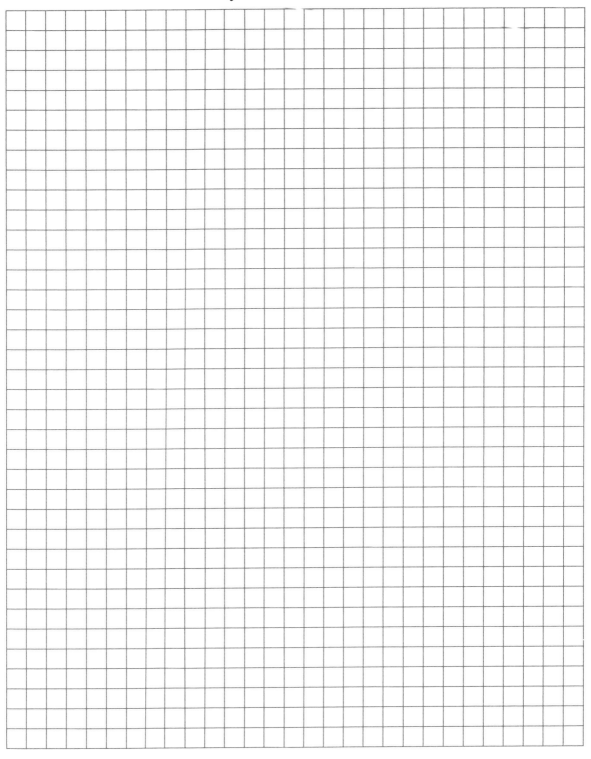

Basil

Basil is native to India and Asia, where its delicious flavor has been used to enhance food for more than 5,000 years. In India, basil is a sacred herb dedicated to Vishnu and Krishna. The Romans considered it a symbol of love, and in some parts of Italy it is still known as kiss-me-Nicholas.

Common basil is a bush plant growing up to 2½ feet in height. The light green, wrinkled leaves are 2 to 3 inches long. The white ½-inch flowers appear along the length of a long stem in July and August.

Basil is available in a variety of shapes, colors, and scents. Miniature, or bush, basil forms a solid compact globe of bright green leaves. Dark opal basil has large, deep purple leaves that make it a striking ornamental garden plant. Green ruffles and purple ruffles are heavily textured. The leaves are very large with ruffled edges in lime green or dark maroon. Scents include lemon, anise, cinnamon, camphor, and clove.

CULTIVATION

Seed can be sown in flats in late spring or early summer or sown directly where the plants are to grow in early summer after the weather has warmed and stabilized. Set the plants 8 to 12 inches apart, or sow seed, in full sun and a rich, moist, well-drained soil. Begin harvesting the leaves while the plant is quite small to promote bushiness, and continue to harvest sprigs throughout the summer. When cold weather threatens, pull up the entire plant and hang upside down in a dark, airy place to dry. Basil tends to discolor if drying is prolonged, and I've found it more satisfactory to strip the leaves from the stems and dry them in the microwave or a very slow oven with the door propped open. Too high a temperature will also cause discoloration. Store basil in airtight containers. Basil can also be frozen.

Basil makes an excellent pot plant for a sunny windowsill to provide you with fresh basil all year long. Sow seeds in a large pot in July or August. Bring indoors before the first frost.

HARVEST

I always allow several plants to set seed so that I can harvest them for next year's planting. Allow the bracts to turn brown before harvesting.

87

Horehound

Perennial—zone 4
Easy

The medicinal qualities of horehound have been valued for thousands of years. Horehound was used to treat just about every known ailment, but its use today is largely confined to cough syrups and cough drops. It is effective in soothing sore throats and coughs and as an expectorant. Horehound candy was also widely available in the early years of this century, and it can still be found in some specialty shops.

Horehound is a very pretty plant with its large, woolly, gray green, crinkled leaves reaching a height of 2 to 3 feet. Try horehound in the flower border as a foil for more gaudy summer flowers. Since bees find horehound attractive, it would be useful planted anywhere you need bees for pollination.

CULTIVATION

Horehound thrives in full sun and dry soil. Since horehound survives on as little as 12 inches of rain a year, when watering, err on the side of too little rather than too much. For best germination, seeds need a cold period. Moisten seeds and place them in the refrigerator for 4 to 8 weeks. Sow seeds ⅛ inch deep in early spring. Thin the seedlings so that they stand 12 to 15 inches apart.

HARVEST

Horehound loses its flavor quickly once picked, and leaves for tea and cough remedies are best used fresh. The leaves can be dried and stored for winter use, but remedies made from these dried leaves require a larger quantity than those made from fresh leaves. Some leaves can be harvested the first year, but it is best to wait until the second year. Cut the leaves just as the flower buds are forming. Remove the leaves from the stems, then chop and dry them as quickly as possible. Store horehound leaves in airtight jars.

Horehound cough drops. Add 1 cup of fresh leaves to 1 pint of water. Bring the water to a boil and steep until the water cools. Strain out leaves. Add 2 cups of sugar (horehound is extremely bitter) or adjust to taste, and boil the mixture until it is thick. Pour the hot mixture into a shallow pan. Allow the mixture to cool until it is comfortable to the touch. Score the candy into bite-size pieces. Let the candy stand until it is cold, and break up the pieces.

september

Date of First Frost _____
Weeks to First Frost _____

Things to Do This Month

- Harvest.
- Fertilize.
- Plant spring bulbs.
- Plant cool-season vegetables: lettuce, spinach, radish.
- Take cuttings of perennials.
- Pot bulbs for forcing.
- Pot herbs.
- As beds empty, add compost, till, and sow winter cover crop.
- Divide overgrown perennials after bloom is over.
- Dig and store summer-blooming bulbs after foliage has ripened.
- Plant seeds of hardy vegetables (such as kale and spinach) in cold frame or other protected bed to winter over.

Sow in Nursery Bed or Cold Frame   **Sow Directly**

FALL PLANTING GUIDE

To determine fall planting dates, you must take into account the fact that the days are getting shorter and extra time will be needed for plants to reach maturity than when planted in the spring. This is known as the *short-day factor* and amounts to about 14 days. The formula is below.

The chart below gives an approximate planting time for various vegetables. Since days to maturity can vary considerably within each type, use the above formula with the information printed on your seed packet to determine the proper planting time for your variety.

	Beets
Days to Maturity	50
Days to Germination	5
Days to Transplant Size	21
Short-Day Factor	14
Days to Count Back from First Frost	70

Guide for Direct Seeding

First Fall Frost _____

Direct Seed	Days to Count Back from First Frost Date
Beets	74 days
Carrots	85–100 days
Chard	69 days
Dill	plant in July
Kale	60 days
Kohlrabi	86 days
Mustard	40 days
Peas	70 days
Radishes	42 days
Radishes, winter	70 days
Rutabaga	105 days
Spinach	64 days
Turnips	63 days

Notes & Observations

Guide for Transplants

From Transplants	Days to Count Back from First Frost Date
Broccoli	95 days
Brussels Sprouts	120 days
Cabbage	99 days
Chinese Cabbage	90 days
Cauliflower	90 days
Collard	94 days
Endive	142 days
Lettuce, head★	96 days
Lettuce, leaf★	76 days

★Lettuce can be sown in flats continuously; so, some are always available for transplanting to the garden.

Perennial Planting & Division Record

Variety	Date Planted	Location	Date Divided

My Garden Plot

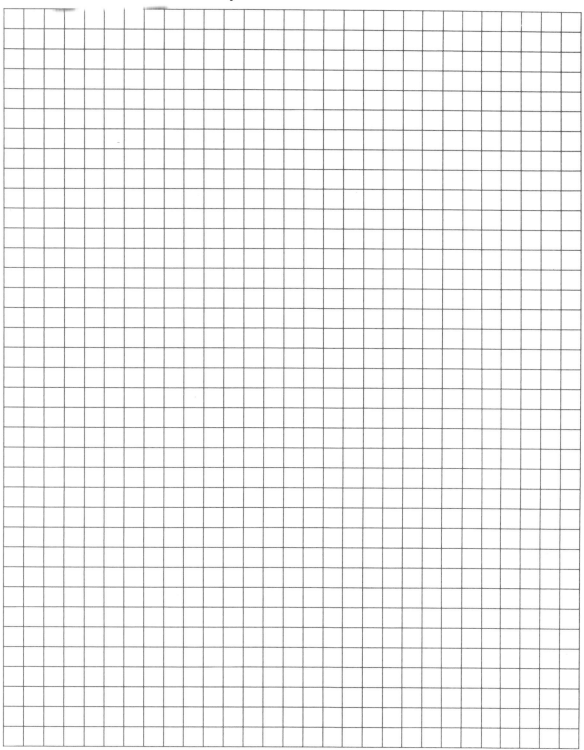

Perennial Planting & Division Record

Variety	Date Planted	Location	Date Divided

Notes & Observations

Perennial Planting & Division Record

Variety	Date Planted	Location	Date Divided

Lavender

Perennial—zones 5 to 8
Moderately difficult

Bury your nose in the gray green leaves, inhale, and the soft heady scent of lavender conjures up images of Old World gentility—courtly gentlemen and lovely ladies in billowy skirts. Lavender seems to have the ability to take you away from the humdrum, everyday world to other times and places. This ability may account for its reputation as a sedative or mild tranquilizer.

Whatever medicinal claims have been made for lavender, its prime use over the millennia has been as a fragrance. Dried lavender flowers are used in potpourris and sachets—not just for their aroma, but also for their ability to repel moths.

CULTIVATION

Lavender prefers full sun and a light, dry, stony, well-drained soil. The preferred method of propagation is to take cuttings from the current year's growth, because lavender does not breed true from seed. Take a healthy shoot and pull down, taking a heel

of the older wood along with the new. Place the cuttings in moist, sandy soil in a shaded bed. The cuttings will remain in the bed for one year, after which they can be transplanted to their permanent location, spacing them 4 to 6 feet apart. Do not allow the plants to flower the first year. Clip the foliage to encourage bushiness. Lavender is actually a shrub, and under good conditions it can spread 5 feet or more in diameter, with a height of 3 feet.

There are numerous varieties of lavender, the hardiest being English lavender, although even these are not reliably winter-hardy and should be protected with a mulch in colder climates.

HARVEST

Harvest flowers and foliage the second year. Flowers can be partially or fully open. Hang in bunches to dry or spread on screens in a shaded area.

Mint

Perennial—zone 5
Easy

The mint family is large, with at least 12 named species, but since the plants readily interbreed, there are numerous hybrids that vary from garden to garden.

Mint has been a cherished garden plant since the day, according to Greek mythology, that Persephone, in a fit of jealous rage, turned the nymph Minthe into a lowly plant to be trodden underfoot. Pluto, unable to change her back, decreed that the more she was trod upon, the sweeter she would smell.

The mints have been used since time immemorial to treat flatulence, abdominal pain, flu, insomnia, fever, headache, toothache, sore throat, insect bites, chapped hands, and bad breath. For most of these applications it truly is effective, since mint, especially peppermint and Japanese mint, contain menthol, the active ingredient in medicinal preparations. And it tastes good, too. Pennyroyal is an effective insect repellant.

With the exception of Corsican mint, which is prostrate in habit, growing only ½ inch high, the mints reach a height of 2 to 3 feet. The leaves are a bright, dark green, oval to pointed, with a crinkly texture. Tiny white, purple, or pink flowers form in whorls around the stem or in terminal spikes.

CULTIVATION

Mints will grow anywhere, but they prefer a moist, rich soil in partial shade. Mint is a rampant grower and will soon take over the bed. So, either confine the mint plant within some type of barrier, or be prepared to pull it out as it spreads. Because mint hybridizes so readily, it is best to begin with started plants, cuttings, or divisions from established plantings. Set the plants 12 to 18 inches apart. To keep them looking their best, cut mints frequently. In late fall, cut them to the ground.

HARVEST

Fresh mint is best; freezing and drying are second-best alternatives. You can begin to pick leaves when the plants come up in the spring and throughout the summer. They make excellent container plants, so pot one or two for winter use.

Date of First Frost _____

Weeks to First Frost _____

Date of Last Frost _____

Weeks to Last Frost _____

Things to Do This Month

- Harvest.
- Plant spring bulbs.
- Begin fall cleanup.
- Take hardwood cuttings.
- Dig up summer bulbs for storage.
- Plant asparagus and berry bushes.
- Begin mulching crops to be wintered over in the ground.

Sow in Nursery Bed or Cold Frame　　　　　　**Sow Directly**

Preserving Log

Variety	Canned		Frozen	
	Pints	Quarts	Pints	Quarts

Notes & Observations

Preserving Log

Variety	Canned		Frozen	
	Pints	Quarts	Pints	Quarts

Notes & Observations

Preserving Log

Variety	Dried	Root Cellar

Notes & Observations

My Garden Plot

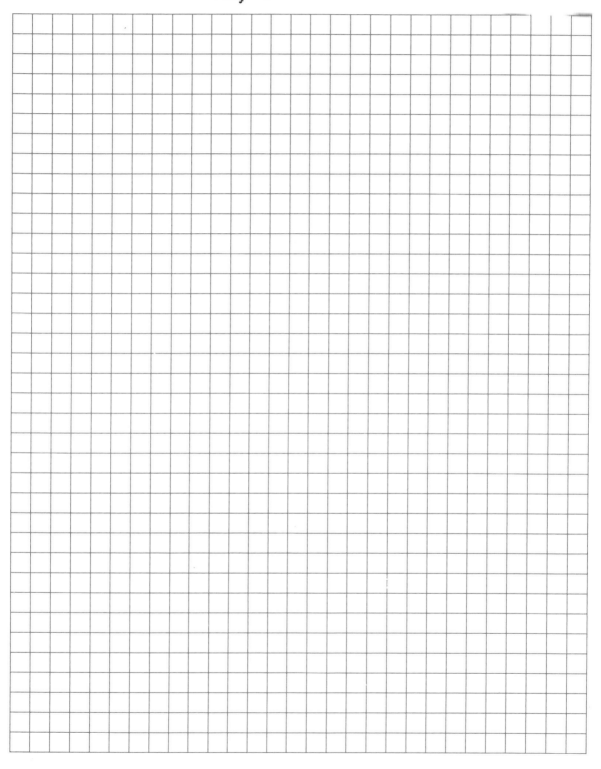

Chives

Perennial—zone 3
Easy

Native to most of the Northern Hemisphere, this member of the onion family has been prized for its mild onion flavor for nearly 5,000 years. The dark green hollow leaves reach a height of 6 to 10 inches. The plant covers itself with ball-shaped lavender flowers in June. If the flowers are cut when they begin to fade, the plant will bloom again later in the summer. This neat, compact plant is highly ornamental and need not be confined to the vegetable or herb garden. It makes a nice edging for the front border of your garden as well as along walkways and paths.

Garlic chives, an equally attractive and carefree plant, has a very mild garlic flavor. It is slightly larger than regular chives and has flatter leaves. The flowers are white.

CULTIVATION

Seeds are slow to germinate, taking two to three weeks. Plant the seeds one-half inch deep in pots or flats, being sure to keep the soil moist. The plants can be set in the garden, 6 to 8 inches apart, when they are four weeks old. The leaves should not be cut the first year. Chives grow wild in moist pastures and along stream banks. So, whether you plant them in the sun or in part shade, be sure they receive enough water to remain moist, not soggy, at all times.

Although a little more costly, it is far easier to buy a plant or two from a nursery. These can be set out any time during the growing season and harvested the same year. That little nursery plant will grow into a nice clump by the end of summer. Once established, the clumps should be dug up and divided every two to three years.

HARVEST

When the plants have reached a height of about 6 inches, you can begin cutting portions of the leaves back to 2 inches. Chives are best when served fresh, but if you want to store them, the best place is the freezer. A more satisfactory alternative is to pot a plant in late summer for winter use.

Dig up a clump of chives and plant it in a container. Chives need a dormant period; leave the container outdoors until the leaves die back and the roots freeze. Bring the container indoors and place it on a sunny windowsill. Plants will sprout in a week or two, and you will have a fresh supply all winter.

Garlic

Garlic, a member of the *liliaceae* family, is a close relative of the onion. It has been under cultivation since pre-biblical times and used as both a vegetable and a medicine. As a medicine, it was used in the Far East to treat high blood pressure and respiratory ailments thousands of years ago. It was used to wash wounds to prevent infection, and during the Middle Ages it was believed that garlic could protect one from the plague.

Interestingly, modern research has substantiated many of the claims made for garlic. It is a potent antiseptic and antibacterial agent. As for preventing plague, garlic has been shown to be effective against some influenza viruses and typhus, staph, and strep bacteria. Research has also shown that garlic will inhibit blood clotting and lower cholesterol levels. All this, and the heavenly flavor it brings to foods, makes garlic a plant one must have in the garden.

Elephant garlic is a milder-flavored form of garlic with much larger cloves.

CULTIVATION

Garlic is native to southern Europe and prefers to grow in full sun. It can be grown from seed, but it is more common to plant the cloves. Separate the garlic bulb into individual cloves, and plant it in a moist, well-drained bed that has been cultivated at least 12 inches deep. In early spring, push the cloves into the loose soil until just barely covered. Space cloves 4 to 6 inches apart in all directions. Cloves can also be planted in the fall, where they will winter over and get an early start in the spring. Elephant garlic is available for planting only in the fall. It requires the same type of soil, but the spacing should be 9 to 12 inches apart. Cut off any flower stalks that appear.

HARVEST

When the leaves begin to turn brown and bend over, it is time to harvest. If they don't do it on their own by August, bend the tops down. Wait a few days and dig up the bulbs. Spread them out in sun or shade to dry for 2 or 3 days. Make sure they are protected if rain threatens. Once the bulbs dry, you can braid the leaves into a rope or wreath or remove the leaves and store them in a cool, dark, dry spot.

november

Date of Last Frost _____
Weeks to Last Frost _____
Set-Out Date _____

Things to Do This Month

- Mulch perennial beds, shrubs, and trees.
- Mulch vegetables that are to be left in the ground.
- Finish preparing beds for spring planting.
- Start hyacinths and paper-white narcissus for indoor blooming.

In the South
Sow seeds of cool-weather plants and those requiring 12 weeks to transplant size.

Plant Indoors in Flats   **Sow Directly**

NATURAL PEST & DISEASE CONTROL

Most organic gardeners are willing to accept some insect damage as long as it doesn't threaten to wipe out an entire crop. In my own garden, I haven't had much of a problem with insects, except for aphids and squash vine borers. Last summer the aphids attacked the Brussels sprouts, but since they only bothered two plants, I let them have those two.

Squash vine borers are something different altogether. Every year, I've tried to grow squash. At most, I've been able to harvest a dozen, then the squash vine borer attacks, and wipes out all the plants. But last summer was different.

Which brings me to the first line of defense in the battle of the bugs: prevention.

Be scrupulous about clean-up in the fall. Any debris left in the garden or orchard provides the perfect breeding conditions for all types of insects. It is especially important to clean up any dropped fruit in the orchard to prevent disease.

Many insects lay their eggs in the soil at the base of the plants, where they winter over and hatch the next spring. Till the soil in the fall to expose these eggs, and again in the spring to expose any larvae that may have hatched.

Practice crop rotation. Never grow the same crop in the same bed two years in a row. This cuts down on disease damage, and any eggs or larvae that have over-wintered will not have their favorite food to feast upon.

With the exception of corn, I do not plant large blocks of the same crop. Instead, I interplant two or more crops in the same location. I learned this trick from my experience with bush beans planted in a large block. Bean beetles went from plant to plant right down the row, defoliating all the plants. Many insects find the smell of marigolds, garlic, and onions offensive and will avoid areas planted with them. Now I either interplant rows of marigolds and onions with the beans, or surround the bed with marigolds. Many herbs are known for their insect-repellant properties. Try interplanting some of the plants listed below to repel insects.

Anise: General repellant. As an insecticide, boil 1 cup of anise leaves and 2 tea bags in 1 pint of water. Strain and cool. Add 2 tablespoons of mineral oil and ¼ cup of soap or 3 tablespoons of mild detergent. Dilute the mixture with 25 percent water when ready to use.

Lemon Balm: General repellant with eggplant, tomatoes, and fruit trees.

Basil: General repellant, especially with tomatoes. Will also repel flies.

Borage: Repels tomato worms.

Calendula: Repels asparagus beetles and worms.

Notes & Observations

Chamomile, Roman. Repels pests that attack the cabbage family. A spray can be made using the same recipe as anise, substituting 6 to 8 chamomile flowers for the leaves.

Catnip: Repels flea beetles and Japanese beetles.

Chives: Repels carrot flies; made into a spray, it prevents applescab on apples and mildew on cucumbers and squash.

Feverfew: Use flowers and leaves to make a pesticide. Add 1 ounce of flowers to 2½ cups of boiling water. Let the mixture steep until cool. Bottle. Use as an insecticide spray, or smooth on the skin to repel mosquitoes and to soothe mosquito bites. The flower head rubbed on mosquito bites makes them stop itching.

Garlic: Deters Japanese beetles and fruit borers. A garlic spray will kill flea beetles.

For a general, all-purpose spray, soak 4 ounces of crushed garlic in mineral oil for several days. Strain and mix oil with a mild soap and water mixture. Store in a sealed container. When ready to use, dilute the resulting mixture with from 10 to 30 parts water.

Here's another garlic spray to try for controlling sucking and chewing insects: Bring 2 cups of water to a boil. Pour the hot water over 8 to 10 crushed garlic cloves and 1 teaspoon of dried hot pepper. Let steep for 15 minutes. Strain and add 2 teaspoons of liquid soap. Use the mixture full strength on woody plants, and dilute 25 percent for annuals and vegetables.

Hyssop: Repels cabbage moths.

Lavender: Repels mosquitoes, flies, and moths.

Oregano: Repels cabbage moths and squash bugs.

Peppermint: Repels white cabbage butterflies. Will also repel fleas when made into a collar for your dog.

Rosemary: Repels carrot flies and some cabbage insects.

Rue: Repels Japanese beetles. To make a spray, take 1 cup of leaves and pour 3 cups of boiling water over them. Let the mixture steep 15 minutes. Strain and bottle.

Southernwood: Repels moths.

Summer Savory: Repels bean beetles.

Tansy: Deters Japanese beetles, striped cucumber beetles, squash bugs, and ants.

Thyme: Repels cabbage worms and cabbage moths.

Trap crops are also an effective deterrent. Insects prefer to feed on certain plants over others, and if one of the preferred plants is planted near a crop that you want to protect, it will lure the insects away. Aphids love nasturtiums, and when these are planted nearby, the aphids will land on the nasturtiums. Radishes lure root maggots away from cabbage crops, dill lures tomato hornworms away from tomatoes, and mustard greens are a good trap crop for harlequin bugs. Be sure to destroy the insects as they gather on the trap crop, or pull up the plants and destroy them to prevent the insects from reproducing.

Timing your plantings to avoid the main bug season is also an effective preventative method. This usually means sowing a week or so earlier or later than you normally would, depending on local conditions.

Modern gardeners are truly fortunate in that we have spun-bonded row covers.

Notes & Observations

These can be applied when the seeds are planted to prevent birds from eating the seeds. As the plants grow, insects can't get to them. The row covers can be left on any plants that do not need pollination, such as lettuce, spinach, cabbages, and so forth, throughout the season. For crops such as tomatoes, squash, peppers, and eggplant, leave the row covers on until the plants flower, then remove the covers so that the plants can be pollinated.

I tend to wait and see if I'm going to have any bug problems before doing anything about it, except for the squash vine borer. The adult moth lays its eggs at the base of the plant. The hatched grubs bore into the stems of squash, cucumbers, pumpkins, and melons, and before long the leaves wilt and the plant dies.

To prevent the moth from laying eggs, when the plants are about 4 inches high, cut squares of aluminum foil and place them under the plants. The foil reflects light and confuses the moth, who is looking for a nice dark place to lay her eggs. I took it a step further, and wrapped the foil loosely around the stem. In case she's not confused, the wrapping on the stem keeps the grubs from penetrating it.

Cutworms can be foiled by cutting a strip of newspaper and wrapping it around the stem of the transplant and extending it down at least 1 inch into the soil. You can also cut cardboard tubes into 3-inch pieces and place them around the stem, being sure the cardboard is buried at least an inch.

Wood ashes, or any scratchy materials placed around the base of plants will discourage slugs. The favorite remedy for catching slugs is to place beer in shallow containers. The slugs drink the beer and drown. If you like to hunt, go out at night, and sprinkle salt on any slugs you find.

A potent insecticide, which should only be used as a last resort to kill all types of insects, is nicotine spray. It kills beneficial as well as pest insects. The nicotine is poisonous to humans and animals, and any application should be done at least a month before harvest. Boil 4 ounces of cigarettes in a gallon of water. Strain. When ready to use, mix 1 part nicotine solution with 2 parts water.

Spider mites can be killed by mixing ¼ cup of buttermilk, 1 cup of flour, and 1 gallon of water.

To lure Japanese beetles, set out a yellow pan with a scent lure, such as geraniol or oil of anise. They are also attracted by a fruit mash of water, sugar, and fruit scraps.

To repel Mexican bean beetles, boil ¼ cup of cedar chips in 1 gallon of water for 2 hours. Strain and dilute with 3 parts water.

To repel corn earworms, apply mineral oil to the tip of the ear with an eyedropper.

Soap and water mix: mix 1 teaspoon of liquid dishwashing soap with 1 cup water.

Sprinkle flour on top of cabbage plants to kill cabbage worms.

Ready-to-use, organic insecticides are available from your local garden center. These include diatomaceous earth, pyrethrins, rotenone, and sabadilla.

Notes & Observations

My Garden Plot

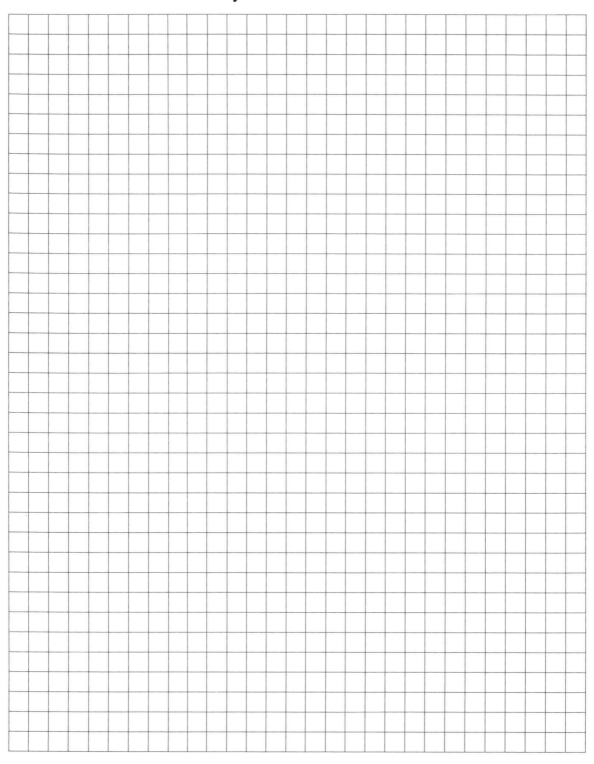

Horseradish

Perennial—zone 5
Easy

Until the 1600s, only the Germans and Danes considered horseradish to have any culinary value. Elsewhere, its use was strictly medicinal, primarily used to treat kidney disorders. A liniment was also made by mixing horseradish with a little water. The mixture generated a gentle heat and helped relieve the pain in stiff and sore muscles. Today, horseradish is considered a culinary herb, and its sharp flavor is the classic condiment for roast beef.

The plant is an herbaceous perennial that reaches 2 to 3 feet in height the second year. The leaves are large, often up to a foot long. Racemes of small white flowers appear in the leaf axils in midsummer.

CULTIVATION

Horseradish is grown from root cuttings. Cut a ½-inch-wide piece of root into 3-inch-long sections. Plant these cuttings in soil that has high organic content. The soil should be loose and well cultivated so that the roots have no obstructions to distort them. The site should be in full sun in the northern regions of the country, but since horseradish prefers cool weather, plant them in a partially shaded location in the South.

Horseradish is a rampant grower, so be careful where you plant it. It will quickly take over the bed unless you take steps to confine it. This can be done by planting horseradish in a five-gallon container, or sink a 12-inch clay pipe into the soil and plant the horseradish in the pipe.

HARVEST

Horseradish can be left in the ground and harvested as needed beginning in late October or early November. You can also dig up the roots, pack them in dry sand, and store them in a cool, dark location. It will also remain fresh for several months in the crisper drawer of your refrigerator.

Sage

Perennial—zones 4 to 8
Easy

Sage, a member of the mint family, is an ancient herb much valued by early civilizations for its medicinal properties. They linked sage to immortality and credited it for increased mental ability. It does have antibacterial properties and, combined with rosemary, can be used to preserve meats, poultry, fish, and condiments. Today, sage is grown primarily for its culinary properties and as a most attractive ornamental in the garden.

Salvia officinalis, or *common sage*, is the one usually grown. Common sage reaches a height of 24 to 30 inches, with grey green, fuzzy leaves. The flowers can be pink, purple, blue, or white and grow in whorls of 4 to 8 flowers at leaf axils in June. There are several other varieties of sage, each with the characteristic flavor but different foliage and growth habits that make them valuable landscape accents. *Blue sage, Salvia clevelandii*, is recommended as a substitute for common sage in cooking and for potpourris. *Pineapple sage* has a strong pineapple fragrance and produces red flowers in the fall. *Golden sage* has striking gold and green variegated leaves that grow up to 18 inches high. *Purple sage* is a compact 18 inches high, with purple foliage. *Tricolor sage* has variegated leaves of cream, purple, and green. *Clary sage* is a biennial that grows 4 to 5 feet high with large, pebbly, gray leaves and beautiful spikes of bluish white and rose flowers.

CULTIVATION

Sage can be started from seed sown indoors in early spring. Seed stores poorly; so, test for germination or plant much more than you need, to be sure that you get the plants you want. Transplant the sage 20 inches apart when the seedlings reach 3 inches high. It will take two years to reach a good size for harvesting. Plants can also be propagated by division or by taking cuttings in the fall. The plants prefer full sun and a well-drained site. They require minimal water, and overwatering or soggy soil will kill them. Trim sage annually to increase its bushiness. Older plants become woody, and the plant should be dug up and divided, discarding the woody portions.

HARVEST

Once established, sage can be harvested any time for fresh use. For drying, cut the stems back, remove the leaves from the stems, and spread them on trays to dry in the shade. Sage can also be frozen.

december

Date of Last Frost _____
Weeks to Last Frost _____
Set-Out Date _____

The 1st real hard frost,
1994 December 1.
1st frost around Nov. 20.

Things to Do This Month

- Check potted bulbs.
- Move plants to bright light.
- Enjoy the holidays!

In the South
Sow seeds requiring 8 weeks to transplant size.

Plant Indoors in Flats   **Sow Directly**

3 Hyacinth bulbs - plant around Christmas ('94)

Sow dill seeds outdoors, will grow in spring.

Seed–Saver's Log

Variety	Date Stored	Quantity	Viability

Notes & Observations

Lavender - *Lavandula latifolia* - easier to grow ↑2ft. } asters, w/ NW corner house??

    - MUNSTEAD STRAIN - 12"

    L. angustifolia (English) ↑2ft

Borage - *Borago officinalis* - ↑2ft.

Sweet Marjoram - *Origanum majorana* ↑2ft.

Winter Savory *Satureja montana* ↑1ft

Summer Savory *Satureja hortensis* ↑18 inches

Feverfew - *Chrysanthemum parthenium* ↑2½ (white)

    Marigolds. INSECT CONTROL

Thyme *Thymus vulgaris* 6"

Chamomile (Roman) *Anthemis nobilis* 2-3"

Chamomile (German) (*Matricaria recutita*) 15-18" (tea - flowers)

Bee Balm (*Melissa officinalis*) 2ft?

Comfrey (*Symphytum x uplandicum* 3-5 ft).

Seed-Saver's Log

Variety	Date Stored	Quantity	Viability

TO STORE SEEDS Pack in glass or metal containers. Add a packet of desiccant to absorb moisture. Store at 32 to 40 degrees Fahrenheit. Seeds can be stored in the refrigerator.

TO CHECK VIABILITY Spread at least 20 seeds on moistened paper towels, wrap them up, and place them in a plastic bag. Set the bag in a warm area. Check seeds daily for signs of sprouting. (Squash seeds can sprout overnight. Parsley may take two or more weeks.) Once seeds begin to sprout, wait a week, and count how many have germinated.

Notes & Observations

My Garden Plot

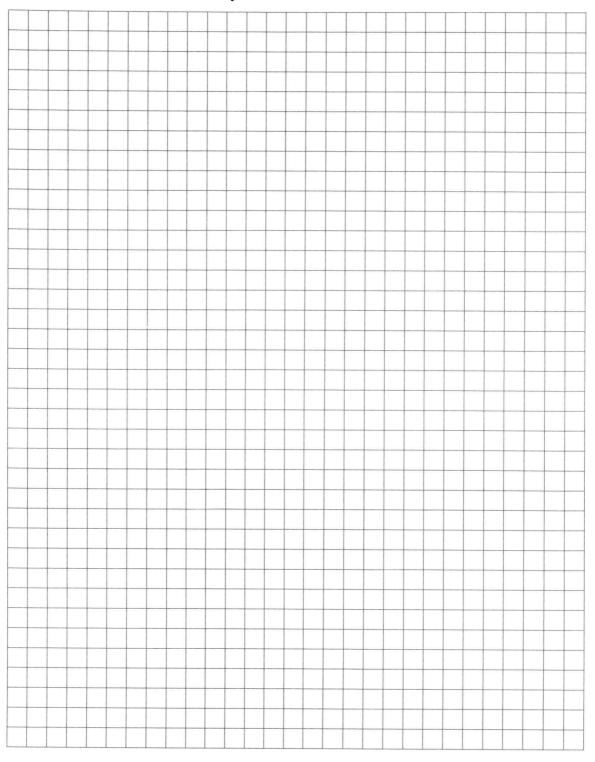

Parsley

Biennial
Difficult to germinate

Parsley is instantly recognizable as that leafy garnish used to accent food on plates in fine restaurants. It's too bad more people don't eat it, since it is packed with vitamins A and C, as well as some B vitamins, vitamin E, calcium, and iron. And it tastes good. I use parsley frequently in salads. Butter and parsley tossed with pasta or new red potatoes makes a very tasty side dish. Chew a few leaves to freshen the breath. It will wipe out the odor of alcohol and even garlic.

In the garden it is an attractive edging plant, growing 6 to 12 inches tall in a mound shape. Most people, when "talking parsley," prefer the flat-leaved Italian varieties, but I like the curled-leaf types. I don't see much difference in taste, and these are prettier plants.

CULTIVATION

Parsley seed is difficult to germinate, taking anywhere from 10 to 45 days, and germination is erratic. To improve germination rates, you can soak the seed for 24 hours before planting. Plant parsley seeds where you want the plants to grow, in a moderately rich, well-drained, moist soil in partial shade or full sun. Or, you can save some aggravation and just buy transplants. Set them out 8 inches apart.

HARVEST

You can begin picking the leaves as soon as the plants are 4 to 6 inches high. Pick the outer leaves, being sure not to damage the growing point at the center of the plant. Parsley is best preserved by freezing. You can also sow seed in a pot for indoor winter use.

Tarragon

Perennial—zone 4
Moderate care

Unlike most herbs, tarragon's distinctive flavor has been used to enhance the flavor of foods rather than for medicinal purposes. Its most famous use is in the making of tarragon vinegar, which, in turn, is an ingredient of mayonnaise and tartar sauce. It also forms a happy marriage with such diverse foodstuffs as asparagus, beef, carrots, fish, game, mushrooms, poultry, rice, and tomatoes, to name a few.

Tarragon (*Artemisia dracunculus*) has been cultivated for at least 2,500 years. Each culture that tarragon entered bestowed a name meaning "dragon upon it" in an attempt to describe the mass of serpentine roots. The French and Spanish call it *estragon*. The term *tarragon* was once, by a confusion of names, applied to the garden dragon, *Dracunculus vulgaris*, an entirely different plant.

There are two species of tarragon— Russian and French. The French type is the one preferred for its rich, full-bodied flavor; Russian tarragon is not used.

French tarragon has long, dark green, lance-shaped leaves of 1 to 4 inches. The plant rarely flowers, but when it does, the flowers are yellow or off-white globes in terminal panicles and usually sterile.

CULTIVATION

Since French tarragon is sterile, it is propagated from cuttings or division. The plant should be divided in spring every three to four years. Those serpentine roots will wrap around themselves and strangle the plant if it is not divided. The divisions should be planted in full sun to partial shade in rich, well-drained soil, about 2 feet apart. The plants should not be allowed to flower. The flowers are usually sterile, and this drains unnecessary energy from the plant. Cuttings can be taken from July to September and set in their permanent location for rooting. Once established, tarragon does not transplant well. In northern climates, the plants should be heavily mulched to keep the roots from freezing.

Tarragon can be grown as a pot plant for winter use. Dig up a mature plant in midsummer, and set it in a large pot. Wrap the pot in plastic, and put it in the refrigerator until fall to force dormancy. In late fall, unwrap the pot and place it in a sunny window that faces south.

HARVEST

Six to eight weeks after setting out the plant, you can begin to harvest tarragon. For use fresh, merely clip a few leaves as needed. For preserving, you can cut the stems back in early summer and again in the fall. Tarragon can be dried by hanging the stems upside down in a warm, dry, dark area. The leaves tend to discolor when dried, and the flavor dissipates quickly. For best results, freeze the leaves.

Zone Map

**Average Annual
Minimum Temperature in Zones**

Temperature (°F)

1:	Below −50°
2:	−40° to −50°
3:	−30° to −40°
4:	−20° to −30°
5:	−10° to −20°
6:	0° to −10°
7:	10° to 0°
8:	20° to 10°
9:	30° to 20°
10:	40° to 30°

Map and Temperature Source: USDA.

**Average Date of Last Spring
Frost in Zones**

1:	June 15
2:	June 10
3:	May 20
4:	May 10
5:	April 20
6:	April 10
7:	March 30
8:	March 10
9:	January 30
10:	No Frost

**Average Date of First Fall
Frost in Zones**

1:	August 1
2:	August 20
3:	September 25
4:	October 1
5:	October 10
6:	October 20
7:	November 10
8:	November 20
9:	December 10
10:	No Frost

WHERE TO FIND IT